ON A COLD WINTER DAY Gillian Lennox almost dies . . . but she is saved by an angel. His hair is golden. His eyes are as violet as her own. And when Gillian comes back from her near-death experience, he comes to her. An invisible guardian only Gillian can see, Angel whispers the secrets of popularity in her ear. Overnight, the once-shy Gillian becomes a sensation, and David, the boy she has loved for years, finally notices her.

But then Angel begins to make bizarre demands, drawing Gillian into a world of risk and dark excitement. At last she has to face the terrifying questions: Who is Angel? What has he brought back from the Other Side? And can she and David find out his secret before it's too late?

DARK ANGEL

THE NIGHT WORLD SERIES

· · · · · · · · · · · · · · · · · · ·

NIGHT WORLD · BOOK FOUR

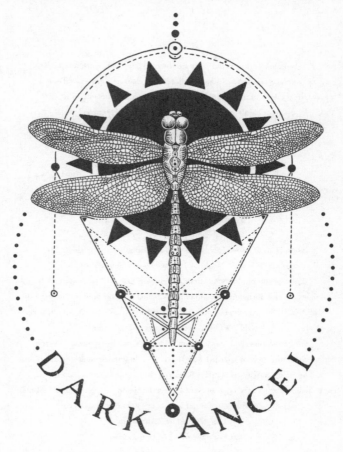

DARK ANGEL

L. J. SMITH

SIMON PULSE
NEW YORK   LONDON   TORONTO   SYDNEY   NEW DELHI

SIMON PULSE

An imprint of Simon & Schuster Children's Publishing Division

1230 Avenue of the Americas, New York, New York 10020

This Simon Pulse hardcover edition April 2017

Text copyright © 1996 by Lisa J. Smith

Cover illustration copyright © 2017 by Neal Williams

Endpaper art of flowers, heart, and sunburst respectively copyright © 2017 by Liliya Shlapak, Nattle, and Ezepov Dmitry/Shutterstock.com

Endpaper art of ornamental flourishes copyright © 2017 by Thinkstock

All rights reserved, including the right of reproduction in whole or in part in any form.

SIMON PULSE and colophon are registered trademarks of Simon & Schuster, Inc.

NIGHT WORLD is a trademark of Lisa J. Smith

For information about special discounts for bulk purchases, please contact Simon & Schuster Special Sales at 1-866-506-1949 or business@simonandschuster.com.

The Simon & Schuster Speakers Bureau can bring authors to your live event. For more information or to book an event contact the Simon & Schuster Speakers Bureau at 1-866-248-3049 or visit our website at www.simonspeakers.com.

Cover designed by Regina Flath

Interior designed by Mike Rosamilia

The text of this book was set in Adobe Garamond.

Manufactured in the United States of America

2 4 6 8 10 9 7 5 3 1

Library of Congress Control Number 2016948192

ISBN 978-1-4814-8944-7 (hc)

ISBN 978-1-4814-8945-4 (eBook)

For Janie, Cathy, and Karen

CHAPTER 1

Gillian Lennox didn't mean to die that day.

She was mad, though. Mad because she had missed her ride home from school, and because she was cold, and because it was two weeks before Christmas and she was very, very lonely.

She walked by the side of the empty road, which was about as winding and hilly as every other country road in south-western Pennsylvania, and viciously kicked offending clumps of snow out of her way.

It was a rotten day. The sky was dull and the snow looked tired. And Amy Nowick, who should have been waiting after Gillian cleaned up her studio art project, had already driven away—with her new boyfriend.

Sure, it must have been an honest mistake. And she wasn't jealous of Amy, she wasn't, even though one week ago they had both been sixteen and never been kissed.

Gillian just wanted to get home.

That was when she heard the crying.

She stopped, looked around. It sounded like a baby—or maybe a cat. It seemed to be coming from the woods.

Her first thought was, Paula Belizer. But that was ridiculous. The little girl who'd disappeared somewhere at the end of this road had been gone for over a year now.

The crying came again. It was thin and far away—as if it were coming from the depths of the woods. This time it sounded more human.

"Hello? Hey, is somebody in there?"

There was no answer. Gillian stared into the dense stand of oak and hickory, trying to see between the gnarled bare trees. It looked uninviting. Scary.

Then she looked up and down the road. Nobody. Hardly surprising—not many cars passed by here.

I am *not* going in there alone, Gillian thought. She was exactly the opposite of the "Oh, it's such a nice day; let's go tromping through the woods" type. Not to mention exactly the opposite of the brave type.

But who else was there? And what else was there to do?

Somebody was in trouble.

She slipped her left arm through her backpack strap, settling it on the center of her back and leaving her hands free. Then she cautiously began to climb the snow-covered ridge that fell away on the other side to the woods.

"Hello?" She felt stupid shouting and not getting any answer. "Hi! Hello!"

Only the crying sound, faint but continuous, somewhere in front of her.

Gillian began to flounder down the ridge. She didn't weigh much, but the crust on the snow was very thin and every step took her ankle deep.

Great, and I'm wearing sneakers. She could feel cold seeping into her feet.

The snow wasn't so deep once she got into the woods. It was white and unbroken beneath the trees—and it gave her an eerie sense of isolation. As if she were in the wilderness.

And it was so *quiet*. The farther Gillian went in, the deeper the silence became. She had to stop and not breathe to hear the crying.

Bear left, she told herself. Keep walking. There's nothing to be scared of!

But she couldn't make herself yell again.

There is something *weird* about this place. . . .

Deeper and deeper into the woods. The road was far behind her now. She crossed fox tracks and bird scratches in the snow—no sign of anything human.

But the crying was right ahead now, and louder. She could hear it clearly.

Okay, up this big ridge. Yes, you *can* do it. Up, up. Never mind if your feet are cold.

As she struggled over the uneven ground, she tried to think comforting thoughts.

Maybe I can write an article about it for the *Viking News* and everyone will admire me. . . . Wait. Is it cool or uncool to rescue somebody? Is saving people too *nice* to be cool?

It was an important question, since Gillian currently had only two ambitions: 1) David Blackburn, and, 2) to be invited to the parties the popular kids were invited to. And both of these depended, in a large part, on being cool.

If she were only popular, if she only felt good about herself, then everything else would follow. It would be so much easier to be a really wonderful person and do something for the world and make something important of her life if she just felt loved and accepted. If she weren't shy and short and immature-looking . . .

She reached the top of the ridge and grabbed at a branch to keep her balance. Then, still hanging on, she let out her breath and looked around.

Nothing to see. Quiet woods leading down to a creek just below.

And nothing to *hear*, either. The crying had stopped.

Oh, don't *do* this to me!

Frustration warmed Gillian up and chased away her fear. She yelled, "Hey—hey, are you still out there? Can you hear me? I'm coming to help you!"

Silence. And then, very faintly, a sound.

Directly ahead.

Oh, my God, Gillian thought. The *creek.*

The kid was in the creek, hanging on to something, getting weaker and weaker. . . .

Gillian was scrambling down the other side of the ridge, slithering, the wet snow adhering to her like lumpy frosting.

Heart pounding, out of breath, she stood on the bank of the creek. Below her, at the edge, she could see fragile ice ledges reaching out like petals over the rushing water. Spray had frozen like diamond drops on overhanging grasses.

But nothing living. Gillian frantically scanned the surface of the dark water.

"Are you there?" she shouted. "Can you hear me?"

Nothing. Rocks in the water. Branches caught against the rocks. The sound of the rushing creek.

"Where *are* you?"

She couldn't hear the crying anymore. The water was too loud.

Maybe the kid had gone under.

Gillian leaned out, looking for a wet head, a shape beneath the surface. She leaned out farther.

And then—a mistake. Some subtle change of balance. Ice under her feet. Her arms were windmilling, but she couldn't get her balance back. . . .

She was flying. Nothing solid anywhere. Too surprised to be frightened.

She hit the water with an icy shock.

CHAPTER 2

Everything was freezing confusion. Her head was under water and she was being tumbled over and over. She couldn't see, couldn't breathe, and she was completely disoriented.

Then her head popped up. She automatically sucked in a huge gasp of air.

Her arms were flailing but they seemed tangled in her backpack. The creek was wide here and the current was very strong. She was being swept downstream, and every other second her mouth seemed to be full of water. Reality was just one desperate, choking attempt to get enough air for the next breath.

And everything was so cold. A cold that was *pain*, not just temperature.

I'm going to die.

Her mind realized this with a sort of numb certainty, but her body was stubborn. It fought almost as if it had a separate brain of its own. It struggled out of her backpack, so that the natural buoyancy of her ski jacket helped keep her head above water. It made her legs kick, trying to stand firm on the bottom.

No good. The creek was only five feet deep in the center, but that was still an inch higher than Gillian's head. She was too small, too weak, and she couldn't get any kind of control over where she was going. And the cold was sapping her strength frighteningly fast. With every second her chances of surviving dropped.

It was as if the creek were a monster that hated her and would never let her go. It slammed her into rocks and swept her on before her hands could get hold of the cold, smooth surfaces. And in a few minutes she was going to be too weak to keep her face above water.

I have to grab something.

Her body was telling her that. It was her only chance.

There. Up ahead, on the left bank, a projecting spit with tree roots. She *had* to get to it. *Kick. Kick.*

She hit and was almost spun past it. But somehow, she was holding on. The roots were thicker than her arms, a huge tangle like slick, icy snakes.

Gillian thrust an arm through a natural loop of the roots, anchoring herself. Oh—yes; she could breathe now. But her body was still in the creek, being sucked away by the water.

She had to get out—but that was impossible. She just barely

had the strength to hold on; her weakened, numb muscles could never pull her up the bank.

At that moment, she was filled with hatred—not for the creek, but for herself. Because she was little and weak and childish and it was going to *kill* her. She was going to die, and it was all happening *right now*, and it was real.

She could never really remember what happened next. Her mind let go and there was nothing but anger and the burning need to get higher. Her legs kicked and scrambled and some dim part of her knew that each impact against the rocks and roots should have hurt. But all that mattered was the desperation that was somehow, inch by inch, getting her numb, water-logged body out of the creek.

And then she was out. She was lying on roots and snow. Her vision was dim; she was gasping, openmouthed, for breath, but she was alive.

Gillian lay there for a long time, not really aware of the cold, her entire body echoing with relief.

I made it! I'll be okay now.

It was only when she tried to get up that she realized how wrong she was.

When she tried to stand, her legs almost folded under her. Her muscles felt like jelly.

And . . . it was *cold*. She was already exhausted and nearly frozen, and her soaking clothes felt as heavy as medieval armor. Her gloves were gone, lost in the creek. Her cap was gone.

With every breath, she seemed to get colder, and suddenly she was racked with waves of violent shivers.

Find the road . . . I have to get to the road. But which way is it?

She'd landed somewhere downstream—but where? How far away was the road now?

Doesn't matter . . . just walk away from the creek, Gillian thought slowly. It was difficult to think at all.

She felt stiff and clumsy and the shivering made it hard to climb over fallen trees and branches. Her red, swollen fingers couldn't close to get handholds.

I'm so cold—why can't I stop shivering?

Dimly, she knew that she was in serious trouble. If she didn't get to the road—*soon*—she wasn't going to survive. But it was more and more difficult to call up a sense of alarm. A strange sort of apathy was coming over her. The gnarled forest seemed like something from a fairy tale.

Stumbling . . . staggering. She had no idea where she was going. Just straight ahead. That was all she could see anyway, the next dark rock protruding from the snow, the next fallen branch to get over or around.

And then suddenly she was on her face. She'd fallen. It seemed to take immense effort to get up again.

It's these clothes . . . they're too heavy. I should take them off.

Again, dimly, she knew that this was wrong. Her brain

was being affected; she was dazed with hypothermia. But the part of her that knew this was far away, separate from her. She fought to make her numbed fingers unzip her ski jacket.

Okay . . . it's off. I can walk better now. . . .

She couldn't walk better. She kept falling. She had been doing this forever, stumbling, falling, getting up. And every time it was a little harder.

Her cords felt like slabs of ice on her legs. She looked at them with distant annoyance and saw that they were covered with adhering snow.

Okay—maybe take those off, too?

She couldn't remember how to work a zipper. She couldn't think at all anymore. The violent waves of shivering were interspersed with pauses now, and the pauses were getting longer.

I guess . . . that's good. I must not be so cold. . . .

I just need a little rest.

While the faraway part of her brain screamed uselessly in protest, Gillian sat down in the snow.

She was in a small clearing. It seemed deserted—not even the footprints of a ground mouse marked the smooth white carpet around her. Above, overhanging branches formed a snowy canopy.

It was a very peaceful place to die.

Gillian's shivering had stopped.

Which meant it was all over now. Her body couldn't warm itself by shivering any longer, and was giving up the fight. Instead, it was trying to move into hibernation. Shutting itself down, reducing breathing and heart rate, conserving the little warmth that was left. Trying to survive until help could come.

Except that no help was coming.

No one knew where she was. It would be hours before her dad got home or her mother was . . . awake. And even then they wouldn't be alarmed that Gillian wasn't there. They'd assume she was with Amy. By the time anyone thought of looking for her it would be far too late.

The faraway part of Gillian's mind knew all this, but it didn't matter. She had reached her physical limits—she couldn't save herself now even if she could have thought of a plan.

Her hands weren't red anymore. They were blue-white. Her muscles were becoming rigid.

At least she no longer felt cold. There was only a vast sense of relief at not having to move. She was so tired. . . .

Her body had begun the process of dying.

White mist filled her mind. She had no sense of time passing. Her metabolism was slowing to a stop. She was becoming a creature of ice, no different from any stump or rock in the frozen wilderness.

I'm in trouble . . . somebody . . . somebody please . . .

Mom . . .

Her last thought was, it's just like going to sleep.

And then, all at once, there was no rigidity, no discomfort.

She felt light and calm and free—and she was floating up near the canopy of snowy boughs.

How wonderful to be warm again! Really warm, as if she were filled with sunshine. Gillian laughed in pleasure.

But where am I? Didn't something just happen—something bad?

On the ground below her there was a huddled figure. Gillian looked at it curiously.

A small girl. Almost hidden by her long pale hair, the strands already covered in fine ice. The girl's face was delicate. Pretty bone structure. But the skin was a terrible flat white—dead-looking.

The eyes were shut, the lashes frosty. Underneath, Gillian knew somehow, the eyes were deep violet.

I get it. I remember. That's me.

The realization didn't bother her. Gillian felt no connection to the huddled thing in the snow. She didn't belong to it anymore.

With a mental shrug, she turned away—

—and she was in a tunnel.

A huge dark place, with the feeling of being vastly complicated somehow. As if space here were folded or twisted—and maybe time, too.

She was rushing through it, flying. Points of light were whizzing by—who could tell how far away in the darkness?

Oh, God, Gillian thought. It's *the* tunnel. This is happening. Right now. To me.

I'm really dead.

And going at warp speed.

Weirder than being dead was being dead with a sense of humor.

Contradictions . . . this felt so real, more real than anything that had ever happened while she was alive. But at the same time, she had a strange sense of unreality. The edges of her self were blurred, as if somehow she were a part of the tunnel and the lights and the motion. She didn't have a distinct body anymore.

Could this all be happening in my head?

With that, for the first time, she felt frightened. Things in her head . . . could be scary. What if she ran into her nightmares, the very things that her subconscious knew terrified her most?

That was when she realized she had no control over where she was going.

And the tunnel had changed. There was a bright light up ahead.

It wasn't blue-white, as she would have expected from movies. It was pale gold, blurred as if she were seeing it through frosty glass, but still unbelievably brilliant.

Isn't it supposed to feel like love or something?

What it felt like—what it made her feel—was awe. The light was so big, so powerful . . . and so Just Plain Bright. It was like looking at the beginning of the universe. And she was rushing toward it so fast—it was filling her vision.

She was in it.

The light encompassed her, surrounded her. Seemed to shine *through* her. She was flying upward through radiance like a swimmer surfacing.

Then the feeling of motion faded. The light was getting less bright—or maybe her eyes were adapting to it.

Shapes solidified around her.

She was in a meadow. The grass was amazing—not just green, but a sort of impossible ultragreen. As if lit up from inside. The sky was the same kind of impossible blue. She was wearing a thin summer dress that billowed around her.

The false color made it seem like a dream. Not to mention the white columns rising at intervals from the grass, supporting nothing.

So this is what happens when you die. And now . . . now, somebody should come meet me. Grandpa Trevor? I'd like to see him walking again.

But no one came. The landscape was beautiful, peaceful, unearthly—and utterly deserted.

Gillian felt anxiety twisting again inside her. Wait, what if this place wasn't—the good place? After all, she hadn't been particularly good in her life. What if this were actually hell?

Or . . . limbo?

Like the place all those spirits who talked to mediums must be from. Creatures from heaven wouldn't say such silly things.

What if she were left here, alone, forever?

As soon as she finished the thought, she wished she hadn't. This seemed to be the kind of place where thoughts—or *fears*—could influence reality.

Wasn't that something rancid she smelled?

And—weren't those voices? Fragments of sentences that seemed to come from the air around her? The kind of nonsense said by people in dreams.

"So white you can't see . . ."

"A time and a half . . ."

"If only I could, girl . . ."

Gillian turned around and around, trying to catch more. Trying to figure out whether or not she was really hearing the words. She had the sudden gut-trembling feeling that the beauty around her could easily come apart at the seams.

Oh, God, let me think good thoughts. *Please.* I wish I hadn't watched so many horror movies. I don't want to see anything terrible—like the ground splitting and hands reaching for me.

And I don't want anyone to meet me—looking like something rotting with bones exposed—after all.

She was in trouble. Even thinking about *not* thinking brought up pictures. And now fear was galloping inside her, and in her mind the bright meadow was turning into a nightmare of darkness and stink and pressure and gibbering mindless things. She was terrified that at any moment she might see a change—

And then she did see one. Something unmistakable. A few feet away from her, above the grass, was a sort of mist of light. It hadn't been there a moment ago. But now it seemed to get brighter as she watched, and to stretch from very far away.

And there was a shape in it, coming toward her.

CHAPTER 3

At first it looked like a speck, then like an insect on a lightbulb, then like a kite. Gillian watched, too frightened to run, until it got close enough for her to realize what it really was.

It was an angel.

Her fear drained away as she stared. The figure seemed to shine, as if it were made of the same light as the mist. It was tall, and had the shape of a perfectly formed human. It was walking, but somehow rushing toward her at the same time.

An angel, Gillian thought, awed. An angel. . . .

And then the mist cleared and the shining faded. The figure was standing on the grass in front of her.

Gillian blinked.

Uh—not an angel, after all. A young guy. Maybe seventeen, a year older than Gillian. And . . . drop dead gorgeous.

He had a face like some ancient Greek sculpture. Classically beautiful. Hair like unburnished gold. Eyes that weren't blue, but violet. Long golden lashes.

And a *terrific* body.

I shouldn't be noticing *that*, Gillian thought, horrified. But it was hard not to. Now that his clothes had stopped shining, she could see that they were ordinary, the kind any guy from earth might wear. Washed and faded jeans and a white T-shirt. And he could easily have done a commercial for those jeans. He was well built without being over-muscly.

His only flaw, if it could be called that, was that his expression was a little *too* uplifted. Almost too sweet for a boy.

Gillian stared. The being looked back. After a moment he spoke.

"Hey, kid," he said, and winked.

Gillian was startled—and mad. Normally, she was shy about speaking to guys, but after all, she was *dead* now, and this person had struck a raw nerve. "Who're you calling kid?" she said indignantly.

He just grinned. "Sorry. No offense."

Confused, Gillian made herself nod politely. Who *was* this person? She'd always heard you had friends or relatives come and meet you. But she'd never seen this guy before in her life.

Anyway, he's definitely not an angel.

"I've come to help you," he said. As if he'd heard her thought.

"Help me?"

"You have a choice to make."

That was when Gillian began to notice the door.

It was right behind the guy, approximately where the mist had been. And it was a door . . . but it wasn't. It was like the luminous outline of a door, drawn very faintly on thin air.

Fear crept back into Gillian's mind. Somehow, without knowing how she knew, she knew the door was important. More important than anything she'd seen so far. Whatever was behind it was—well, maybe beyond comprehension.

A different place. Where all the laws she knew didn't apply.

Not necessarily bad. Just so powerful and so different that it was scary. Good can be scary, too.

That's the *real* gateway, she thought. Go through that door and you don't come back. And even though part of her longed desperately to see what was behind it, she was still so frightened that she felt dizzy.

"The thing is, it wasn't *actually* your time," the guy with the golden-blond hair said quietly.

Oh, yes, I should have known. That's the cliché, Gillian thought. But she thought it weakly. Looking at that door, she didn't have room left inside for cute remarks.

She swallowed, blinking to clear her eyes.

"But here you are. A mistake, but one we have to deal with. In these cases, we usually leave the decision up to the individual."

"You're saying I can choose whether or not I die."

"To put it sort of loosely."

"It's just up to *me*?"

"That's right." He tilted his head slightly. "You might want to think your life over at this point."

Gillian blinked. Then she took a few steps away from him and stared across the supernaturally green grass. She tried to think about her life.

If you'd asked me this morning if I wanted to stay alive, there would have been no question. But now . . .

Now it felt a little like being rejected. As if she weren't good enough. And besides, seeing that she'd come this far . . . did she really want to go back?

It's not as if I were anybody special there. Not smart like Amy, a straight A student. Not brave. Not talented.

Well, what else is there? What would I be going back to?

Her mom—drinking every day, asleep by the time Gillian got home. Her dad and the constant arguments. The loneliness she knew she'd be facing now that Amy had a boyfriend. The longing for things she could never have, like David Blackburn with his quizzical smile. Like popularity and love and acceptance. Like having people think she was interesting and—and mature.

Come on. There's got to be something good back there.

"Cup Noodles?" the guy's voice said.

Gillian turned toward him. "Huh?"

"You like those. Especially on a cold day when you come inside. Cats. The way babies smell. Cinnamon toast with lots of butter, like your mom used to make it when she still got up in the morning. Bad monster movies."

Gillian choked. She'd never told anyone about most of those things. "How do you *know* all that?"

He smiled. He really had an extraordinary smile. "Eh, we see a lot up here." Then he sobered. "And don't *you* want to see more? Of life, I mean. Isn't there anything left for you to do?"

Everything was left for her to do. She'd never accomplished anything worthwhile.

But I didn't have much time, a small wimpy voice inside her protested. To be quashed immediately by a stern, steady voice. *You think that's an excuse? Nobody knows how much time they've got. You had plenty of minutes, and you wasted most of them.*

"Then don't you think you'd better go back and try again?" the guy said, in a gentle, prodding voice. "See if you can do a better job?"

Yes. All at once, Gillian was filled with the same burning she'd felt when she got out of the creek. A sense of revelation and of purpose. She could do that. She could change completely, turn her life in a whole new direction.

Besides, there were her parents to consider. No matter how bad things were between them now, it could only make it worse if their daughter suddenly died. They'd blame each other. And Amy would get one of her guilt complexes for not waiting to drive Gillian home from school. . . .

The thought brought a little grim satisfaction. Gillian tried to quell it. She had the feeling the guy was listening.

But she *did* have a new perspective on life. A sudden feeling that it was terribly precious, and that the worst thing you could do was waste it.

She looked at the guy. "I want to go back."

He nodded. Gave the smile again. "I thought maybe you would." His voice was so warm now. There was a quality in it that was like—what? Pure love? Infinite understanding?

A tone that was to sound what perfect light was to vision.

He held out a hand. "Time to go, Gillian," he said gently. His eyes were the deepest violet imaginable.

Gillian hesitated just an instant, then reached toward him.

She never actually touched his hand, not in a physical way. Just as her fingers seemed about to meet his, she felt a tingling shock and there was a flash. Then he was gone and Gillian had several odd impressions all at once.

The first was of being . . . unfixed. Detached from her surroundings. A falling feeling.

The second was of something coming at her.

It was coming very fast from some direction she couldn't point to. A place that wasn't defined by up or down or left or right. And it felt huge and winged, the way a hawk's shadow must feel to a mouse.

Gillian had a wild impulse to duck.

But it wasn't necessary. She was moving herself, falling away.

Rushing backward through the tunnel, leaving the meadow—and whatever was coming at her—behind. The huge thing had only registered for an instant on her senses, and now, whizzing back through the darkness, she forgot about it.

Later, she would realize what a mistake this had been.

For now, time seemed compressed. She was alone in the tunnel, being pulled down like water down a drain. She tried to look between her feet to see where she was going, and saw something like a deep well beneath her.

At the bottom of the well was a circle of light, like the view backwards through a telescope. And in the circle, very tiny, was a girl's body lying on the snow.

My body, Gillian thought—and then, before she had time to feel any emotion, the bottom of the well was rushing up toward her. The tiny body was bigger and bigger. She felt a tugging pressure. She was being sucked into it—too fast.

Way too fast. She had no control. She fit perfectly in the body, like a hand slipping into a mitten, but the jolt knocked her out.

Oooh . . . something hurts.

Gillian opened her eyes—or tried to. It was as hard as doing a chin-up. On the second or third attempt she managed to get them open a crack.

Whiteness everywhere. Dazzling. Blinding.

Where . . . ? Is it snow?

What am I doing lying down in the snow?

Images came to her. The creek. Icy water. Climbing out. Falling. Being so cold . . .

After that . . . she couldn't remember. But now she knew what hurt. Everything.

I can't move.

Her muscles were clenched tight as steel. But she knew she couldn't stay here. If she did, she'd . . .

Memory burst through her.

I died already.

Strangely, the realization gave her strength. She actually managed to sit up. As she did, she heard a cracking sound. Her clothes were glazed with solid ice.

Somehow she got to her feet.

She shouldn't have been able to do it. Her body had been cold enough to shut down earlier, and since then she'd been lying in the snow. By all the laws of nature, she should be frozen now.

But she was standing. She could even shuffle a step forward.

Only to realize she had no idea which way to go.

She still didn't know where the road was. Worse, it would be getting dark soon. When that happened, she wouldn't even be able to see her own tracks. She could walk in circles in the woods until her body gave out again.

"See that white oak tree? Go around it to the right."

The voice was behind her left ear. Gillian turned that way

as sharply as her rigid muscles would allow, even though she knew she wouldn't see anything.

She recognized the voice. But it was so much warmer and gentler now.

"You came back with me."

"Sure." Once again the voice was filled with that impossible warmth, that perfect love. "You don't think I'd just leave you to wander around until you froze again, do you? Now head for that tree, kid."

After that came a long time of stumbling and staggering, over branches, around trees, on and on. It seemed to last forever, but always there was the voice in Gillian's ear, guiding her, encouraging her. It kept her moving when she thought she couldn't possibly go another step.

And then, at last, the voice said, "Just up this ridge and you'll find the road."

In a dreamlike state, Gillian climbed the ridge.

And there it was. The road. In the last light before darkness, Gillian could see it meandering down a hill.

But it was still almost a mile to her house, and she couldn't go any farther.

"You don't have to," the voice said gently. "Look up the road."

Gillian saw headlights.

"Now just get in the middle of the road and wave."

Gillian stumbled out and waved like a mechanical doll.

The headlights were coming, blinding her. Then she realized that they were slowing.

"We did it," she gasped, dimly aware that she was speaking out loud. "They're stopping!"

"Of course they're stopping. You did a great job. You'll be all right now."

There was no mistaking the note of finality.

The car was stopped now. The driver's side door was opening. Gillian could see a dark figure beyond the glare of the headlights. But in that instant what she felt was distress.

"Wait, don't leave me. I don't even know who you are—"

For a brief moment, she was once again enfolded by love and understanding.

"Just call me Angel."

Then the voice was gone, and all Gillian could feel was anguish.

"What are you doing out— Hey, are you okay?" The new voice broke through Gillian's emptiness. She had been standing rigidly in the headlights; now she blinked and tried to focus on the figure coming toward her.

"God, of course you're not okay. Look at you. You're Gillian, aren't you? You live on my street."

It was David Blackburn.

The knowledge surged through her like a shock, and it drove all the strange hallucinations she'd been having out of her mind.

It really *was* David, as close as he'd ever been to her.

Dark hair. A lean face that still had traces of a summer tan. Cheekbones to die for and eyes to drown in. A certain elegance of carriage. And that half-friendly, half-quizzical smile. . . .

Except that he wasn't smiling now. He looked shocked and worried.

Gillian couldn't get a single word out. She just stared at him from under the icy curtain of her hair.

"What hap— No, never mind. We've got to get you warm."

At school he was thought of as a tough guy, an independent rebel. But, now, without any hesitation, the tough guy scooped her up in his arms.

Confusion flashed through Gillian, then embarrassment— but underneath it all was something much stronger. An odd bedrock sense of safety. David was warm and solid and she knew instinctively that she could trust him. She could stop fighting now and relax.

"Put this on . . . watch your head . . . here, use this for your hair." David was somehow getting everything done at once without hurrying. Capable and kind. Gillian found herself inside the car, wrapped in his sheepskin jacket, with an old towel around her shoulders. Heat blasted from the vents as David gunned the engine.

It was wonderful to be able to rest without being afraid it would kill her. Bliss not to be surrounded by cold, even if the hot air didn't seem to warm her. The worn beige interior of the Mustang seemed like paradise.

And David—well, no, he didn't look like an angel. More like a knight, especially the kind who went out in disguise and rescued people.

Gillian was beginning to feel very fuzzy.

"I thought I'd take a dip," she said, between chattering teeth. She was shivering again.

"What?"

"You asked what happened. I was a little hot, so I jumped in the creek."

He laughed out loud. "Huh. You're brave." Then he glanced at her sideways with keen eyes and added, "What *really* happened?"

He thinks I'm brave! A glow better than the heated air enveloped Gillian.

"I slipped," she said. "I went into the woods, and when I got to the creek—" Suddenly, she remembered why she'd gone into the woods. She'd forgotten it since the fall had put her own life in danger, but now she seemed to hear that faint, pathetic cry all over again.

"Oh, my God," she said, struggling to sit upright. "Stop the car."

CHAPTER 4

David went on driving. He didn't even pause. "We're almost home."

They were nearing the turn onto Meadowcroft Road. Gillian tried to grab for one of the brown hands on the steering wheel, and then looked at her own hand, perplexed. Her fingers felt like blocks of wood.

"You have to stop," she said, settling for volume. "There's a kid lost in those woods. That's why I went in; I heard this sound like crying. It was coming from somewhere right near the creek. We've got to go back there. Come on, *stop!*"

"Hey, hey, calm down," he said. "You know what I bet you heard? A long-eared owl. They roost around here, and they make this noise like a moan, *oo-oo-oo.*"

Gillian didn't think so. "I was walking home from school. It wasn't dark enough for an owl to be out."

"Okay, a mourning dove. Goes *oh-ah, whoo, whoo.* Or a cat;

they can sound like kids sometimes. Look," he added almost savagely, as she opened her mouth again, "when we get you home, we can call the Houghton police, and they can check things out. But I am *not* letting a lit—a girl freeze just because she's got more guts than smarts."

For a moment, Gillian had an intense longing to let him continue to believe she had either guts *or* smarts. But she said, "It's not that. It's just—I've already been through so much to try to find that kid. I almost died—I think I *did* die. I mean—well, I didn't die, but I got pretty cold, and—and things happened, and I realized how important life is. . . ." She floundered to a shivering stop. What was she *saying*? Now he was going to think she was a nutcase. And anyway, all that stuff must have been a dream. She couldn't make it seem real while sitting in a Mustang with her head wrapped in a towel.

But David flashed her a glance of startled recognition.

"You almost died?" He looked back at the road, turning the car onto Hazel Street, where they both lived. "That happened to me once. When I was little, I had to have this operation—"

He broke off as the Mustang skidded on some ice. In a moment he was in control again and turning into Gillian's driveway.

It happened to you, too?

David parked and was out of the car before Gillian could gather herself to speak.

Then he was opening her door, reaching for her.

"Gotta get all this ridiculous stuff out of the way," he said, pushing her hair back as if it were a curtain of cobwebs. Something about the way he said it made Gillian think he liked her hair.

She peered up at him through a gap in the curtain. His eyes were dark brown and normally looked almost hawkish, but just now, as their gazes met, they changed. They looked startled and wondering. As if he saw something in her eyes that surprised him and struck a chord.

Gillian felt a flutter of wonder herself. I don't think he's really tough at all, she thought, as something like a spark seemed to flash between them. He's not so different from me; he's—

She was wracked by a sudden bout of shivers.

David blinked and shook his head. "We've got to get you inside," he muttered.

And then, still shivering, she was in the air. Bobbing, being carried up the path to her house.

"You shouldn't be walking to school in the winter," David said. "I'll drive you from now on."

Gillian was struck speechless. On the one hand, she should probably tell him she didn't walk *every* day. On the other hand, who was she kidding? Just the thought of him giving her a ride was enough to make her heart beat wildly.

Between that and the novel feeling of being carried, it

wasn't until he was opening the front door that Gillian remembered her mother.

Then she panicked.

Oh, God, I can't let David see her—but maybe it'll be all right.

If there was a smell of food cooking, that meant it was okay. If not, it was one of Mom's bad days.

There was no smell of food as David stepped into the dim hallway. And no sign of life—all the downstairs lights were off. The house was cold and echoing and Gillian knew she had to get David out.

But how? He was carrying her farther in, asking, "Your parents aren't home?"

"I guess not. Dad doesn't get home until seven most nights." It wasn't *exactly* a lie. Gillian just prayed her mom would stay put in the bedroom until David left.

"I'll be okay now," she said hastily, not even caring if she sounded rude or ungrateful. Anything to make him *go*. "I can take care of myself, and—and I'm okay."

"The he . . . eck you are," David said. It was the longest drawn out "heck" Gillian had ever heard.

He doesn't want to swear around me. That's cute.

"You need to get thawed out, fast. Where's a bathtub?"

Gillian automatically lifted a stiff arm to point down the side hall, then dropped it. "Now, wait a minute—"

He was already there. He put her on her feet, then disappeared into the bathroom to turn on the water.

Gillian cast an anguished glance upstairs. Just *stay put*, Mom. Stay asleep.

"You've got to get in there and stay for at least twenty minutes," David said, reappearing. "Then we can see if you need to go to the hospital at Houghton."

That made Gillian remember something. "The police—"

"Yeah, right, I'll call them. As soon as you're in the tub." He reached out and plucked at her dripping, ice-crusted sweater. "Can you get this off okay? Do your fingers work?"

"Um . . ." Her fingers didn't work; they were still blocks of wood. Frost-nipped at least, she thought, peering at them. But there was no way he was going to undress her, and there was also no way she was going to call her mother. "Um . . ."

"Uh, turn around," David said. He pulled at her sweater again. "Okay, I've got my eyes shut. Now—"

"No," Gillian said, holding her elbows firmly against her sides.

They stood, confused and indecisive, until they were saved by an interruption, a voice from the main hallway.

"What are you *doing* to her?" the voice said.

Gillian turned and looked around David. It was Tanya Jun, David's girlfriend.

Tanya was wearing a velveteen cap perched on her glossy dark hair and a Christmas sweater with metallic threads woven in. She had almond-shaped gray eyes and a mouth with firm lips molded over white teeth. Gillian always thought of her as a future corporate executive.

"I saw your car out there," the future executive said to David, "and the front door of the house was open." She looked levelheaded, suspicious, and a little bit as if she doubted David's sanity. David looked back and forth between her and Gillian and fumbled for an explanation.

"There's nothing going on. I picked her up on Hillcrest Road. She was—well, *look* at her. She fell in the creek and she's frozen."

"I see," Tanya said, still calmly. She gave Gillian a quick assessing glance, then turned back to David. "She doesn't look too bad. You go to the kitchen and make some hot chocolate. Or hot water with Jell-O in it, something with sugar. I'll take care of her."

"And the police," Gillian called after David's disappearing back. She didn't exactly want to look Tanya in the face.

Tanya was a senior like David, in the class ahead of Gillian at Rachel Carson High School. Gillian feared her, admired her, and hated her, in about that order.

"Into the bathroom," Tanya said. Once Gillian was in, she helped her undress, stripping off the clinging, icy-wet clothes and dropping them in the sink. Everything she did was brisk and efficient, and Gillian could almost see sparks fly from her fingers.

Gillian was too miserable to protest at being stripped

naked by somebody with the bedside manner of a female prison guard or an extremely strict nanny. She huddled, feeling small and shivering in her bare skin, and then lunged for the tub as soon as Tanya was done.

The water felt scalding. Gillian could feel her eyes get huge and she clenched her teeth on a yell. It probably felt so hot because *she* was so cold. Breathing through her nose, she forced herself to submerge to the shoulders.

"All right," Tanya said on the other side of the coral-colored shower curtain. "I'll go up and get you some dry clothes to put on."

"No!" Gillian said, shooting half out of the water. Not upstairs, not where her mom was, not where her *room* was.

But the bathroom door was already shutting with a decisive click. Tanya wasn't the kind of person you said no to.

Gillian sat, immobilized by panic and horror, until a fountain of burning pain drove everything else out of her mind.

It started in her fingers and toes and shot upward, a white-hot searing that meant her frozen flesh was coming back to life. All she could do was sit rigid, breathe raggedly through her nose, and try to endure it.

And eventually, it did get better. Her white, wrinkled skin turned dark blue, and then mottled, and then red. The searing subsided to a tingling. Gillian could move and think again.

She could hear, too. There were voices outside the bath-room in the hallway. The door didn't even muffle them.

Tanya's voice: "Here, I'll hold it. I'll take it to her in a min-ute." In a mutter: "I'm not sure she can drink and float at the same time."

David's voice: "Come on, give her a break. She's just a kid."

"Oh, really? Just how old do you think she is?"

"Huh? I don't know. Maybe thirteen?"

An explosive snort from Tanya.

"Fourteen? Twelve?"

"David, she goes to our school. She's a junior."

"Really?" David sounded startled and bewildered. "Nah, I think she goes to P.B."

Pearl S. Buck was the junior high. Gillian sat staring at the bathtub faucet without seeing it.

"She's in our *biology* class," Tanya's voice said, edging toward open impatience. "She sits at the back and never opens her mouth." The voice added, "I can see why you thought she was younger, though. Her bedroom's knee-deep in stuffed animals. And the wallpaper's little flowers. And look at these pajamas. Little bears."

Gillian's insides felt hotter than her fingers had been at their most painful. Tanya had seen her room, which was the same as it had been since Gillian was ten years old, because there wasn't money for new curtains and wallpaper and there wasn't any more storage space in the garage to put her beloved animals away. Tanya was making fun of her pajamas. In front of David.

And David . . . thought she was a little kid. That was why he'd offered to drive her to school. He'd meant the junior high. He'd been nice because he felt *sorry* for her.

Two tears squeezed out of Gillian's eyes. She was trembling inside, boiling with anger and hurt and humiliation. . . .

Crinch.

It was a sound as loud as a rifle report, but high and crystalline—and drawn out. Something between a crash and a crunch and the sound of glass splintering under boots.

Gillian jumped as if she'd been shot, sat frozen a moment, then pulled the moisture-beaded shower curtain aside and poked her head out.

At the same instant the bathroom door flew open.

"What was that?" Tanya said sharply.

Gillian shook her head. She wanted to say, "You tell *me*," but she was too frightened of Tanya.

Tanya looked around the bathroom, spied the steamed-up mirror, and frowned. She reached across the sink to wipe it with her hand—and yelped.

"Ow!" She cursed, staring at her hand. Gillian could see the brightness of blood.

"What the—?" Tanya picked up a washcloth and swiped the mirror. She did it again. She stepped back and stared.

From the tub, Gillian was staring, too.

The mirror was broken. Or, not broken, cracked. But it wasn't cracked as if something had hit it. There was no point of impact, with lines of shattering running out.

Instead, it was cracked evenly from top to bottom, side to side. Every inch was covered with a lattice of fine lines. It almost looked purposeful, as if it were a frosted-glass design.

"David! Get in here!" Tanya said, ignoring Gillian. After a moment the door stirred and Gillian had a steamy distorted glimpse of David's face in the mirror.

"Do you see this? How can something like this happen?" Tanya was saying.

David grimaced and shrugged. "Heat? Cold? I don't know." He glanced hesitantly in Gillian's direction, just long enough to locate her face surrounded by the coral shower curtain.

"You okay?" he said, addressing himself to a white towel rack on the far wall.

Gillian couldn't say anything. Her throat was too tight and tears were welling up again. But when Tanya looked at her, she nodded.

"All right, forget it. Let's get you changed." Tanya turned away from the mirror. David melted back out of the bathroom.

"Make sure her fingers and everything are working all right," he said distantly.

"I'm fine," Gillian said when she was alone with Tanya. "Everything's fine." She wiggled her fingers, which were tender but functioning. All she cared about right now was getting Tanya to go away. "I can dress myself."

Please don't let me cry in front of her.

She retreated behind the shower curtain again and made a splashing noise. "You guys can leave now."

Half a sigh from Tanya, who was undoubtedly thinking Gillian was ungrateful. "All right," she said. "Your clothes and your chocolate are right here. Is there somebody you want me to call—?"

"No! My parents—my dad will be here any minute. I'm *fine.*" Then she shut her eyes and counted, breath held.

And, blessedly, there were the sounds of Tanya moving away. Both Tanya and David calling goodbyes. Then silence.

Stiffly, Gillian pulled herself upright, almost falling down when she tried to step out of the bathtub.

She put on her pajamas and walked slowly out of the bathroom, moving like an old woman. She didn't even glance at the broken mirror.

She tried to be quiet going up the stairs. But just as she reached her bedroom, the door at the end of the upstairs hall swung open.

Her mother was standing there, a long coat wrapped around her, fuzzy fleece-lined slippers on her feet. Her hair, a darker blond than Gillian's, was uncombed.

"What's going on? I heard noise. Where's your father?"

Not "Whass goin' on? Whersh your father?" But close.

"It's not even seven yet, Mom. I got wet coming home. I'm going to bed." The bare minimum of sentences to communicate the necessary information.

Her mother frowned. "Honey—"

"'Night, Mom."

Gillian hurried into her bedroom before her mother could ask any more questions.

She fell on her bed and gathered an armful of stuffed animals in the bend of her elbow. They were solid and friendly and filled her arm. Gillian curled herself around them and bit down on plush.

And now, at last, she could cry. All the hurts of her mind and body merged and she sobbed out loud, wet cheek on the velveteen head of her best bear.

She wished she'd never come back. She wanted the bright meadow with the impossibly green grass, even if it had been a dream. She wanted everyone to be sorry because she was dead.

All her realizations about life being important were nonsense. Life was a giant hoax. She *couldn't* change herself and live in a completely new direction. There was no new start. No hope.

And I don't care, she thought. I just want to die. Oh, why did I get *made* if it was just for this? There's got to be someplace I belong, something I'm meant to do that's different. Because I don't fit in this world, in this life. And if there isn't something more, I'd rather be dead. I want to dream something else.

She cried until she was numb and exhausted and fell into a deadly still sleep without knowing it.

When she woke up hours later, there was a strange light in her room.

CHAPTER 5

Actually, it wasn't the light she noticed first. It was an eerie feeling that some . . . presence was in her room with her.

She'd had the feeling before, waking up to feel that *something* had just left, maybe even in the instant it had taken her to open her eyes. And that while asleep, she'd been on the verge of some great discovery about the world, something that was lost as soon as she woke.

But tonight, the feeling *stayed*. And as she stared around the room, feeling dazed and stupid and leaden, she slowly realized that the light was wrong.

She'd forgotten to close the curtains, and moonlight was streaming into the room. It had the thin blue translucence of new snow. But in one corner of Gillian's room, by the gilded Italian chest of drawers, the light seemed to have pooled. Coalesced. Concentrated. As if reflecting off a mirror.

There wasn't any mirror.

Gillian sat up slowly. Her sinuses were stuffed up and her eyes felt like hard-boiled eggs. She breathed through her mouth and tried to make sense of what was in the corner.

It looked like . . . a pillar. A misty pillar of light. And instead of fading as she woke up, it seemed to be getting brighter.

An ache had taken hold of Gillian's throat. The light was so beautiful . . . and almost familiar. It reminded her of the tunnel and the meadow and . . .

Oh.

She knew now.

It was different to be seeing this when she wasn't dead. Then, she'd accepted strange things the way you accept them in dreams, without ordinary logic or disbelief interfering.

But now she stared as the light got brighter and brighter, and felt her whole skin tingling and tears pooling in her eyes. She could hardly breathe. She didn't know what to do.

How do you greet an angel in the ordinary world?

The light continued to get brighter, just as it had in the meadow. And now she could see the shape in it, walking toward her and rushing at the same time. Still brighter—dazzling and pulsating—until she had to shut her eyes and saw red and gold after images like shooting stars.

When she squinted her eyes back open, he was there.

Awe caught at Gillian's throat again. He was so beautiful that it was frightening. Face pale, with traces of the light still lingering in his features. Hair like filaments of gold. Strong shoulders, tall but graceful body, every line pure and proud and *different* from any human. He looked more different now than he had in the meadow. Against the drab and ordinary background of Gillian's room, he burned like a torch.

Gillian slid off her bed to kneel on the floor. It was an automatic reflex.

"Don't do that." The voice was like silver fire. And then— it changed. Became somehow more ordinary, like a normal human voice. "Here, does this help?"

Gillian, staring at the carpet, saw the light that was glinting off a stray safety pin fade a bit. When she tilted her eyes up, the angel looked more ordinary, too. Not as luminous. More like just an impossibly beautiful teenage guy.

"I don't want to scare you," he said. He smiled.

"Yeah," Gillian whispered. It was all she could get out.

"Are you scared?"

"Yeah."

The angel made a frustrated circling motion with one arm. "I can go through all the gobbledygook: be not afraid, I mean you no harm, all that—but it's such a waste of time, don't you think?" He peered at her. "Aw, come on, kid, you died earlier today. Yesterday. This isn't really all that strange in comparison. You can deal."

"Yeah." Gillian blinked. "Yeah," she said with more conviction, nodding.

"Take a deep breath, get up—"

"Yeah."

"—say something different. . . ."

Gillian got up. She perched on the edge of her bed. He was right, she *could* deal. So it hadn't been a dream. She had really died, and there really were angels, and now one was in the room with her, looking almost solid except at the edges. And he had come to . . .

"Why did you come here?" she said.

He made a noise that, if he hadn't been an angel, Gillian would have called a snort. "You don't think I ever really left, do you?" he said chidingly. "I mean, think about it. How did you manage to recover from freezing without even needing to go to the hospital? You were in severe hypothermia, you know. The worst. You were facing pulmonary edema, ventricular fibrillation, the loss of a few of your bits. . . ." He wiggled his fingers and waggled his feet. That was when Gillian realized he was standing several inches off the floor. "You were in bad shape, kid. But you got out of it without even frostbite."

Gillian looked down at her own ten pink fingers. They were tinglingly oversensitive, but she didn't have even one blood blister. "You saved me."

He gave a half grin and looked sheepish. "Well, it's my job."

"To help people."

"To help *you*."

A barely acknowledged hope was forming in Gillian's mind. He never really left her; it was his job to help her. That sounded like . . . Could he be . . .

Oh, God, no, it was too corny. Not to mention presumptuous.

He was looking sheepish again. "Yeah. I don't know how to put it, either. But it *is* true, actually. Did you know that most people *think* they have one even when they don't? Somebody did a poll, and 'most people have an inner certainty that there is some particular, individual spirit watching over them.' The New Agers call us spirit guides. The Hawaiians call us *aumakua.* . . ."

"You're a guardian angel," Gillian whispered.

"Yeah. *Your* guardian angel. And I'm here to help you find your heart's desire."

"I—" Gillian's throat closed.

It was too much to believe. She wasn't worthy. She should have been a better person so that she would *deserve* some of the happiness that suddenly spread out in front of her.

But then a cold feeling of reality set in. She *wasn't* a better person, and although she was sure enlightenment and whatever else an angel thought your heart's desire was, was terrific, well . . . in her case . . .

She swallowed. "Look," she said grimly. "The things I need help with—well, they're not exactly the kinds of things angels are likely to know about."

"Heh." He grinned. He leaned over in a position that would have unbalanced an ordinary person and waved an imaginary something over her head. "You *shall* go to the ball, Cinderella."

A wand. Gillian looked at him. "Now you're my fairy godmother?"

"Yeah. But watch the sarcasm, kid." He changed to a floating position, his arms clasping his knees, and looked her dead in the eye. "How about if I say I know your heart's desire is for David Blackburn to fall madly in love with you and for everyone at school to think you're totally hot?"

Heat swept up Gillian's face. Her heart was beating out the slow, hard thumps of embarrassment—and excitement. When he said it out loud like that, it sounded extremely shallow . . . and extremely, extremely desirable.

"And you could *help* with that?" she choked out.

"Believe it or not, Ripley."

"But you're an *angel.*"

He templed his fingers. "The paths to enlightenment are many, Grasshopper. Grasshopper? Maybe I should call you Dragonfly. You *are* sort of iridescent. There're lots of other insects, but Dung Beetle sounds sort of insulting. . . ."

I've got a guardian angel who sounds like Robin Williams, Gillian thought. It was wonderful. She started to giggle uncontrollably, on the edge of tears.

"Of course, there's a condition," the angel said, dropping

his fingers. He looked at her seriously. His eyes were like the violet-blue at the bottom of a flame.

Gillian gulped, took a scared breath. "What?"

"You have to trust me."

"That's *it*?"

"Sometimes it won't be so easy."

"Look." Gillian laughed, gulped again, steadied herself. She looked away from his eyes, focusing on the graceful body that was floating in midair. "Look, after all I've seen . . . after you saved my life—and my *bits* . . . how could I not trust you?" She said it again quietly. "How could I ever not trust you?"

He nodded. Winked. "Okay," he said. "Let's prove it."

"Huh?" Slowly the feeling of awed incredulity was fading. It was beginning to seem almost normal to talk to this magical being.

"Let's prove it. Get some scissors."

"Scissors?"

Gillian stared at the angel. He stared back.

"I don't even know where any scissors are."

"Drawer to the left of the silverware drawer in the kitchen. A big sharp pair." He grinned like Little Red Riding Hood's grandmother.

Gillian wasn't afraid. She didn't decide not to be, she simply wasn't.

"Okay," she said and went down to get the scissors. The angel went with her, floating just behind her shoulder. At the bottom of the stairs were two Abyssinian cats, curled up head to toe like the yin-yang symbol. They were fast asleep. Gillian nudged one gently with one toe, and it opened sleepy crescents of eyes.

And then it was off like a flash—both cats were. Streaking down the side hall, falling over each other, skidding on the hardwood floor. Gillian watched with her mouth open.

"Balaam's ass," the angel said wisely.

"I *beg* your pardon?" For a moment Gillian thought she was being insulted.

"I mean, animals can see us."

"But they were *scared*. All their fur—I've never seen them like that before."

"Well, they may not understand what I am. It happens sometimes. Come on, let's get the scissors."

Gillian stared down the side hall for a moment, then obeyed.

"Now what?" she said as she brought the scissors back to her room.

"Go in the bathroom."

Gillian went into the little bathroom that adjoined her bedroom and flicked on the light. She licked dry lips.

"And now?" she said, trying to sound flippant. "Do I cut off a finger?"

"No. Just your hair."

In the mirror over the sink, Gillian saw her own jaw drop. She couldn't see the angel, though, so she turned around.

"Cut my *hair*? *Off*?"

"Off. You hide behind it too much. You have to show the world that you're not hiding anymore."

"But—" Gillian raised protective hands, looking back in the mirror. She saw herself, pale, delicate boned, with eyes like wood violets—peering out from a curtain of hair.

So maybe he had a point. But to go into the world *naked*, without anything to duck behind, with her face exposed . . .

"You said you trusted me," the angel said quietly.

Gillian chanced a look at *him*. His face was stern and there was something in his eyes that almost scared her. Something unknowable and cold, as if he were withdrawing from her.

"It's the way to prove yourself," he said. "It's like taking a vow. If you can do this part, you're brave enough to do what it takes to get your heart's desire." He paused deliberately. "But, of course, if you're not brave enough, if you want me to go away . . ."

"*No,*" Gillian said. Most of what he was saying made sense, and as for what she didn't understand—well, she would have to have faith.

I can do this.

To show that she was serious, she took the open scissors, bracketed the pale blond curtain at a level with her ear, and squeezed them shut. Her hair just folded around the scissors.

"Okay." The angel was laughing. "Hold on to the hair at the bottom and *pull*. And try less hair."

He sounded like himself again: warm and teasing and loving—helpful. Gillian let out her breath, gave a wobbly smile, and devoted herself to the horrible and fascinating business of cutting off long blond chunks.

When she was done, she had a silky blond cap. Short. It was shorter than Amy's hair, almost as short as J. Z. Oberlin's hair, the girl at school who worked as a model and looked like a Calvin Klein ad. It was *really* short.

"Look in the mirror," the angel said, although Gillian was already looking. "What do you see?"

"Somebody with a bad haircut?"

"Wrong. You see somebody who's brave. Strong. Out there. Unique. Individualist. And, incidentally, gorgeous."

"Oh, please." But she *did* look different. Under the ragged St. Joan bob, her cheekbones seemed to stand out more; she looked older, more sophisticated. And there was color in her cheeks.

"But it's still all uneven."

"We can get it smoothed out tomorrow. The important thing is that you took the first step yourself. By the way, you'd better learn to stop blushing. A girl as beautiful as you has to get used to compliments."

"You're a funny kind of angel."

"I told you, it's part of the job. Now let's see what you've got in your closet."

An hour later, Gillian was in bed again. This time, under

the covers. She was tired, dazed, and very happy.

"Sleep fast," the angel said. "You've got a big day tomorrow."

"Yes. But wait." Gillian tried to keep her eyes open. "There were some things I forgot to ask you."

"Ask."

"That crying I heard in the woods—the reason I went in. Was it a kid? And are they okay?"

There was a brief pause before he answered. "That information is classified. But don't worry," he added. "Nobody's hurt—now."

Gillian opened one eye at him, but it was clear he wasn't going to say any more. "Okay," she said reluctantly. "And the other thing was—I *still* don't know what to call you."

"I told you. Angel."

Gillian smiled, and was immediately struck by a jaw-cracking yawn. "Okay. Angel." She opened her eyes again. "Wait. One more thing . . ."

But she couldn't think of it. There had been some other mystery she'd wanted to ask about, something that had to do with Tanya, with Tanya and blood. But she couldn't summon it up.

Oh, well. She'd remember later. "I just wanted to say—thank you."

He snorted. "You can say it anytime. Get this through your head, kid: I'm not going anywhere. I'll be here tomorrow morning." He began to hum a Blind Melon song. "'I'll always be there when you wake. . . .' Yeah, yeah, yeah."

Gillian felt warm, protected . . . loved. She fell asleep smiling.

The next morning she woke early and spent a long time in the bathroom. She came down the stairs feeling self-conscious and light-headed—literally. With her hair gone, her neck felt as if it were floating. She braced herself as she walked into the kitchen.

Neither of her parents was there, even though her father was usually having breakfast by now. Instead, a girl with dark hair was sitting at the kitchen table, bent closely over a calculus textbook.

"Amy!"

Amy glanced up and blinked. She squinted, blinked again, then jumped up, standing an inch taller than Gillian. She moved forward, her eyes huge.

Then she screamed.

CHAPTER 6

Your hair!" Amy screamed. "Gillian, your *hair*! What
did you *do* to it?"

Amy's own hair was short, cropped close in back
and full in front. She had large, limpid blue eyes that always looked
as if she were about to cry, because she was nearsighted but couldn't
wear contacts and wouldn't wear glasses. Her face was sweet and
usually anxious; just now it looked more anxious than normal.

Gillian put a self-conscious hand to her head. "Don't you
like it?"

"I don't know! It's gone!"

"This is true."

"But *why*?"

"Calm down, Amy." (If this is the way everybody's going
to react, I think I'm in trouble.) Gillian had discovered that she
could talk to Angel without moving her lips and that he could
answer in her head. It was convenient.

(Tell her you cut it because it froze. That ought to flip her guilt circuits.) Angel's voice sounded the same as it did when she could see him. Soft, wry, distinctly his. It seemed to be located just behind her left ear.

"I had to cut it because it was frozen," Gillian said. "It broke off," she added brightly, inspired.

Amy's blue eyes got even wider with horror. She looked stricken. "Oh, my God, Gillian—" Then she cocked her head and frowned. "Actually, I don't think that's possible," she said. "I think it'd stay pliable even frozen. Unless, like, you dipped it in liquid nitrogen. . . ."

"Whatever," Gillian said grimly. "I did it. Listen, I've got it slicked back behind my ears right now, but the ends are sort of uneven. Can you smooth them out a little?"

"I can try," Amy said doubtfully.

Gillian sat down, pulling together the neck of the rose-colored bathrobe she was wearing over her clothes. She handed Amy the scissors. "Got a comb?"

"Yes. Oh, Gillian, I was trying to tell you. I'm so sorry about yesterday. I just forgot—but it's all my fault—and you almost *died*!" The comb quivered against the back of Gillian's neck.

"Wait a minute. How did you find out about that?"

"Eugene heard it from Steffi Lockhart's little brother, and I think Steffi heard it from David Blackburn. Did he really save you? That's so incredibly romantic."

"Yeah, sort of." (Uh, what do I tell people about that? What do I tell them about the whole thing?)

(The truth. Up to a point. Just leave me and the near-death stuff out.)

"I've been thinking all morning," Amy was saying, "and I realized that I've been an absolute pig this last week. I don't deserve to be called a best friend. And I want you to know that I'm sorry, and that things are going to be different now. I came to pick *you* up first, and then we're going to get Eugene."

(Oh, joy.)

(Be nice, dragonfly. She's trying. Say thank you.)

Gillian shrugged. It didn't seem to matter much *what* Amy did, now that she had Angel. But she said, "Thanks, Amy," and held still as the cold scissors went *snip* behind her ear.

"You're so sweet," Amy murmured. "I thought you'd be all mad. But you're such a good person. I felt so terrible, thinking about you alone out there, freezing, and being so brave, trying to save a little kid—"

"Did they *find* a kid?" Gillian interrupted.

"Huh? No, I don't think so. Nobody was talking about anything like that last night. And I haven't heard about any kid being missing, either."

(Told you, dragonfly. Are you satisfied now?)

(Yes, I am. Sorry.)

"But it was still brave," Amy said. "Your mom thinks so, too."

"My mom's up?"

"She went to the store. She said she'd be back in a few minutes." Amy stepped back and looked at Gillian, scissors held in the air. "You know, I'm not sure I should be doing this. . . ."

Before Gillian could summon up a reply, she heard the sound of the front door opening and the rustling of paper bags. Then her mother appeared, her cheeks red with cold. She had two grocery bags in her arms.

"Hi, girls," she began, and broke off. She focused on Gillian's hair. Her mouth fell open.

"Don't drop the bags," Gillian said. She tried to sound careless, but her stomach was clenched like a fist. Her neck felt stiff and unnatural as she held very still. "Do you like it?"

"I—I—" Gillian's mother put the bags on the counter. "Amy . . . did you have to cut it *all*?"

"Amy didn't do it. I did it last night. I just got tired of it long—" (And getting all wet and icy) "—and getting all wet and icy. So I cut it. So do you like it, or not?"

"I don't know," her mother said slowly. "You look so much older. Like a Parisian model."

Gillian glowed.

"Well." Her mother shook her head slightly. "Now that it's done—here, let me shape it a little. Just touch up the ends." She took the scissors from Amy.

(I'm going to be bald when this is finished!)

(No, you're not, kid. She knows what she's doing.)

And, strangely, there was something comforting about

feeling her mother gently wield the scissors. About her mother's scent, which was fresh like lavender soap, without any hint of the terrible alcohol smell. It reminded Gillian of the old days, when her mom taught at the junior college and was up every morning and never had uncombed hair or bloodshot eyes. Before the fights started, before her mom had to go to the hospital.

Her mother seemed to feel it, too. She gave Gillian's shoulder a pat as she whisked a bit of cut hair away. "I got fresh bread. I'll make cinnamon toast and hot chocolate." Another pat, and then she spoke with careful calm. "Are you sure you're all right? You must have been . . . pretty cold last night. We can call Dr. Kaczmarek if you want; it wouldn't take a minute."

"No, I'm fine. Really. But where's Daddy? Did he already go to work?"

There was a pause, then her mother said, still calmly, "Your father left last night."

"Dad left?" (Dad *left*?)

(It happened last night while you were asleep.)

(A *lot* seems to have happened last night while I was asleep.)

(The world's kind of that way, dragonfly. It keeps on going even when you're not paying attention.)

"Anyway, we'll talk about it later," her mother said. A final pat. "There, that's perfect. You're beautiful, even if you don't look like my little girl anymore. You'd better bundle up, though; it's pretty cold out this morning."

"I'm already dressed." The moment had come, and Gillian

didn't really care if she shocked her mother now or not. Her father had left again—and if that wasn't unusual, it was still upsetting. The closeness with her mother had been spoiled, and she didn't want cinnamon toast anymore.

Gillian stepped to the middle of the kitchen and shrugged off the pink bathrobe.

She was wearing black hipsters and a black camisole. Over it was a sheer black shirt, worn loose. She had on flat black boots and a black watch, and that was *all* she had on.

"Gillian."

Amy and her mother were staring.

Gillian stood defiantly.

"But you never wear black," her mother said weakly.

Gillian knew. It had taken a long time to cull these things from the forgotten hinterlands of her closet. The camisole was from Great-Grandma Elspeth, two Christmases ago, and had still had the price tag attached.

"Didn't you sort of forget to put on a sweater on top?" Amy suggested.

(Stand your ground, kid. You look terrific.)

"No, I didn't forget. I'm going to wear a coat outside, of course. How do I *look*?"

Amy swallowed. "Well—great. Extremely hot. But kind of scary."

Gillian's mother lifted her hands and dropped them. "I don't really know you anymore."

(Hooray!)

(Yup, kid. Perfect.)

Gillian was happy enough to give her mother a flying kiss. "Come on, Amy! We'd better get moving if we're going to pick up Eugene." She dragged the other girl behind her like the tail of a comet. Her mother followed, calling worriedly about breakfast.

"Give us something to take with us. Where's that old black coat I never wore? The fancy one you got me for church. Never mind, I found it."

In three minutes she and Amy were on the porch.

"Wait," Gillian said. She fished through the black canvas bag she was carrying in place of a backpack and came up with a small compact and a tube of lipstick. "I almost forgot."

She put on the lipstick. It was red, not orange-red or blue-red, but *red* red, the color of holly berries or Christmas ribbon. That shiny, too. It made her lips look fuller, somehow, almost pouty. Gillian pursed her lips, considered her image, then kissed the compact mirror lightly and snapped it shut.

Amy was staring again. "Gillian . . . *what* is going *on*? What's happened to you?"

"Come on, we're going to be late."

"The outfit just makes you look like you're going out to burgle something, but that lipstick makes you look . . . *bad*. Like a girl with a reputation."

"Good."

"Gillian! You're scaring me. There's something—" She caught Gillian's arm and peered into her eyes. "Something about you—*around* you—oh, I don't know what I'm talking about! But it's different and it's dark and it's *not good.*"

She was so genuinely shaken that for a moment Gillian was frightened herself. A quick stab of fear like the flick of a knife in her stomach. Amy was neurotic, sure, but she wasn't the type to hallucinate. What if—

(Angel—)

A horn honked.

Startled, Gillian turned. Right at the edge of the driveway, behind Amy's Geo, was a somewhat battered but still proud tan Mustang. A dark head was sticking out the window.

"Standing me up?" David Blackburn called.

"What—is—*that*?" Amy breathed.

Gillian waved to David—after a sharp nudge from Angel. "I think it's called a car," she said to Amy. "I forgot. He said he'd drive me to school. So—I guess I should go with him. See you!"

It only made sense to go with David; after all, he *had* asked first. Besides, Amy's driving was life threatening; she sped like a maniac and wove all over the road because she couldn't see without her glasses.

It should have been satisfying. After all, yesterday Amy had stood *her* up for a guy—and a guy like Eugene Elfred. But right this moment Gillian was too scared to be smug.

This was it. David was going to see her new self. And it was all happening too fast.

(Angel, what if I faint? What if I throw up? *That's* going to make a great first impression, isn't it?)

(Keep breathing, kid. Breathe. Breathe. Not that fast. Now smile.)

Gillian couldn't quite manage a smile as she opened the car door. Suddenly she felt exposed. What if David thought she was cheap or even freakish? Like a little girl dressed up in her mom's clothes?

And her hair—all at once she remembered how David had touched it yesterday. What if he *hated* it?

Trying to breathe, she slipped into the car. Her coat came open as she sat down. She could hardly make herself look toward the driver's seat.

But when she did, her breath stopped completely. David was wearing a look that she'd never seen on any guy's face before, at least not directed toward her. She'd seen it, occasionally, when guys were looking at other girls, girls at school like Steffi Lockhart or J. Z. Oberlin. A stricken gaze, a compulsive movement of the throat, an expression that almost made you sorry for them. An "I'm lying down and I don't care if you walk on me, babe," expression.

David was looking at *her* that way.

Immediately all her fear, including the little stab induced by Amy, was swept away. Her heart was still pounding and little waves of adrenaline were still going through her, but now what it felt like was excitement. Heady, buoyant anticipation. As if she had started on the roller coaster ride of her life.

David actually had to shake himself before he remembered to put the car in gear. And then he kept sneaking glances at her out of the side of his eye.

"You did something to your . . . and your . . ." He made a vague motion near his own head. Gillian's gaze was caught by his hand, which was strong, brown, long-fingered, and handsome.

"Yeah, I cut my hair," she said. She meant to sound careless and sophisticated, but it came out shaky, with a little laugh at the end. She tried again. "I figured I didn't want to look too young."

"Ouch." He made a face. "That's my fault, isn't it? You overheard that stuff yesterday. What Tanya and I said."

(Tell him you've been thinking of doing it for a while.)

"Yeah, but I've been thinking of doing it for a while now," Gillian said. "It's no big deal."

David glanced at her as if to say *he* disagreed with that. But it wasn't a disapproving glance. It was more like electrified awe . . . and a sort of discovery that seemed to grow every time he looked at her.

"And I never saw you at school?" he muttered. "I must've been blind."

"Sorry?"

"No, nothing. *I'm* sorry." He drove in silence for a while. Gillian forced herself to stare out the window and realized they were on Hillcrest Road. Strange how different the landscape looked today. Yesterday it had been lonely and desolate; this morning it seemed harmless, and the snow looked soft and comfortable, like old cushions.

"Listen," David said abruptly. He broke off and shook his head. And then he did something that absolutely amazed Gillian. He pulled the car to the side of the road—or at least as far to the side as he could get it—they were still in the flow of traffic—and parked it.

"There's something I have to say."

Gillian's heart now seemed to be beating everywhere, in her throat and her fingertips and her ears. She had a dreamlike sensation that her body wasn't solid anymore, that she was just a floating mass of heartbeat. Her vision shimmered. She was . . . waiting.

But what David said was unexpected. "Do you remember the first time we met?"

"I—yes." Of course she did. Four years ago; she'd been twelve and tiny for her age. She'd been lying on the ground beside her house, making snow angels. Kind of childish, sure, but in those days a stretch of new snow had affected her that way. And while she was lying on her back, arms out, making the imprint of the angel's wings, a tree branch above her decided to shrug off its load of snow. Suddenly her face was covered in damp, closely packed coldness and she couldn't breathe. She came up spluttering and gasping.

And found herself steadied. Something was holding her, wiping her face gently. The first thing she saw when she got her vision back was a brown hand and a lean brown wrist. Then a face came into focus: high strong bones and dark, mischievous eyes.

"I'm David Blackburn. I just moved in over there," the boy said. He was wiping her face with his fingers. "You'd better be careful, snow princess. Next time I might not be around."

Looking up at him, Gillian had felt her heart explode and leak out of her chest.

And she'd walked away on air, even though he'd patted her head after releasing her. She was in love.

"Well, back then, I sort of got the wrong impression," David was saying. "I thought you were a lot younger and more—well, more *fragile* than you are." There was a pause, and then he said wonderingly, not quite looking at her, "But, it's like, there's so much more to you. I started realizing that yesterday."

Gillian understood. David didn't have a reputation for being wild for nothing. He liked girls who were bold, dashing, out there. If he were a knight, he wouldn't fall in love with the pampered princess back at the castle. He'd fall in love with a female knight, or maybe a robber, somebody who could share the Adventure with him, who'd be just as tough as he was.

Of course he had a strong protective streak. That was why he rescued maidens in distress. But he didn't *go* for the maidens who needed rescuing.

"And now," David was saying. "Now, I mean, you're . . ." He held his hands up in a *whoa* motion. He wasn't looking at her at all.

In a moment of perfect bliss, Gillian thought, I'm cool.

"You're kind of incredible," David said. "And I feel *really* stupid for not noticing that before."

Gillian couldn't breathe. There was something between her and David—a kind of quivering electricity. The air was so thick with it that she felt pressure all over her. She had never been so awake before, but at the same time she felt as if most of the world was insubstantial. Only she and David were real.

And the voice in her head seemed very far away. (Uh, dragonfly, we've got company. Incoming.)

Gillian couldn't move. A car drove by, swerving to avoid the Mustang. Gillian couldn't see well through the Mustang's steamed-up windows, but she thought faces were looking at her.

David didn't seem to notice the car at all. He was still staring at the gearshift, and when he spoke his voice was very quiet. "So I guess what I'm saying is, I'm sorry if anything I said hurt your feelings. And—I see you now."

He raised his head. And Gillian suddenly realized he was going to kiss her.

CHAPTER 7

Gillian felt triumph, wild excitement—and something deeper. An emotion she couldn't describe because there weren't any ordinary words for it. David was looking at her, and it was almost as if she could see *through* his dark eyes. As if she could see inside him . . . see the way things looked to him . . .

What she felt was a little like discovery and a little like déjà vu and a little like waking up and suddenly realizing it's Christmas. Or like being a kid lost in a strange place, cold and bewildered, and then suddenly hearing your mother's voice. But it really wasn't like any of those things; it was *more*. Unexpected welcome . . . strange recognition . . . the shock of belonging . . .

She couldn't quite put it all together, because there was nothing like it in her experience. She'd never *heard* of anything like this. But she had the feeling that when David kissed her, she'd figure it all out and it would be the revelation of her life.

It was going to happen—now. He was moving closer to her, not fast, but as if slowly compelled by something he couldn't control. Gillian had to look down, but she didn't move back or turn her face away. He was close enough now that she could hear his breath and feel him. Her eyes shut of their own accord.

She waited to feel the touch of warmth on her lips. . . .

And then something in her mind stirred. A tiny whisper, so far back that she could barely hear it, and she couldn't tell where it came from.

Tanya.

The shock went through Gillian like ice on bare skin. Part of her tried to ignore it, but she was already pulling away, putting a hand up, turning to stare at the window.

Not *out* the window. It was too steamed up now to see anything outside. They were in their own cocoon of whiteness.

Gillian said, "I *can't*. I mean, not like this. I mean—it isn't fair, because you already—and you haven't . . . I mean . . . *Tanya*."

"I know." David sounded as if *he'd* been hit with ice on bare skin, or as if he'd come up from deep water and was looking around dazedly. "I mean, you're right. I don't know what I was . . . It just—it was like I forgot . . . Look, I'm sure that sounds stupid. You don't believe me."

"I do believe you." At least he sounded as incoherent as she did. He wouldn't think she was a total fool; her facade wasn't broken.

"I'm not that kind of guy. I mean, it looks like I am, right

here, it looks exactly like I am. But I'm *not*. I mean I never—
I'm not like Bruce Faber. I don't do that. I made a promise to
Tanya and . . ."

Oh, God, Gillian thought. And then a sort of inward
scream: (Help!)

(I was wondering when you'd remember me.)

(He made her a promise!)

(I'm sure he did. They've been going together a while.)

(But that's *terrible*!)

(No, it's admirable. What a guy. Now say you've got to
get to school.)

(I can't. I can't *think*. How are we going to—)

(School first.)

Dully, Gillian said, "I guess we'd better get moving."

"Yeah." There was a pause, and then David put the car
in gear.

They drove in silence, and Gillian sank deeper and deeper
into depression. She'd thought it would be so easy—just show
David her new self and everything would fall into place. But
it wasn't like that. He couldn't just dump Tanya.

(Don't worry about it, kid. I have a cunning plan.)

(But *what*?)

(I'll tell you when it's time.)

(Angel—are you *mad* at me? Because I forgot about you?)

(Of course not. I'm here to arrange things so you can
forget me.)

(Then—because I forgot about Tanya for a while? I don't want to do anything that's wrong. . . .)

(I'm not mad! Heads-up. You're there.)

Gillian couldn't push away the feeling that he *was* mad, though. Or at least surprised. As if something unexpected had happened.

But she didn't have time to dwell on it. She had to get out of David's car and gather herself and face the high school.

"I guess—I'll see you later," David said as she reached for the door handle. His voice made it a question.

"Yeah. Later," Gillian said. She didn't have the energy for anything more. She glanced back—once—to see him staring at the steering wheel.

She could see people staring at *her* as she walked to the school building. It was a new sensation and it gave her a spasm of anxiety.

Were they laughing at her? Did she look silly, was she walking *wrong* somehow?

(Just breathe and walk.) Angel's voice sounded amused. (Breathe—walk—head up—breathe. . . .)

Gillian somehow got through halls and up stairs to her U.S. history class without meeting another student's eyes once.

There, arriving just as the bell rang, she realized she had a problem. Her history textbook, along with all her notes, was floating somewhere down toward West Virginia.

With relief, she caught Amy's eye and headed toward the back of the classroom.

"Can I share your book? My whole backpack went in the creek." She was a little afraid Amy might be miffed or jealous at the way she'd run off with David, but Amy didn't seem to be either. She seemed more—awed—as if Gillian were some force like a tornado that you might fear, but that you couldn't get mad at.

"Sure." Amy waited until Gillian had scooted her desk closer, then whispered, "How come it took you so long to get to school? What were you and David *doing*?"

Gillian rummaged for a pen. "How do you know we weren't picking up Tanya?"

"Because Tanya was here at school looking for *David*."

Gillian's heart flip-flopped. She pretended to be very interested in history.

But she gradually noticed that some of the other students were looking at her. Especially the boys. It was the sort of look she'd never imagined getting from a boy.

But these were all juniors, and none of them was in the really popular clique. All that would change in Gillian's next class, biology. Half a dozen of the most popular kids would be there. David would be there—and Tanya.

Gillian felt, with a sudden chill, that she might not really care anymore. What did it matter what other people thought of her if she couldn't have David? But she had a fundamental faith in Angel. Somehow things *had to* work out—if she just stayed calm and played her part.

When the bell rang, she hurried away from Amy's questioning eyes and into the bathroom. She needed a moment to herself.

(Do something to your lipstick. It seems to have gone away somehow.) Angel sounded as puzzled as any human boy.

Gillian fixed the lipstick. She ran a comb through her hair. She was somewhat reassured by the sight of herself in the mirror. The girl there wasn't Gillian at all, but a slender, insubstantial femme fatale sheathed like a dagger in black. The girl's hair was silky, the palest of all possible golds. Her violet eyes were subtly shadowed so they looked mysterious, haunting. Her mouth was soft, red, and full: perfect, like the mouth of a model in a lipstick commercial. Against the stark black of her clothing, her skin had the slightly translucent look of apple blossoms.

She's beautiful, Gillian thought. And then to Angel: (I mean, I am. But I need . . . a Look, don't you think? An expression for when people are staring at me. Like, am I Bored or Slightly Amused or Aloof or Completely Oblivious or what?)

(How about Thoughtful? As if you've got your own inner world to pay attention to. It's true, you know. You do.)

Gillian was pleased. Thoughtful, absorbed in herself, listening to the music of the spheres—or the music of Angel's voice. She could do that. She settled the canvas bag on her shoulder and started toward her locker.

(Uh, where are you going?)

(To get my biology book. I still have that.)

(No, you don't.)

Gillian maintained her Thoughtful expression, while noting that heads turned as she walked down the hall. (Yes, I do.)

(No, you don't. Due to circumstances entirely beyond your control, you lost your biology book and all your notes. You need to sit with somebody else and share *his.*)

Gillian blinked. (I—*oh.* Oh, yeah, you're right. I lost my biology book.)

The door of the biology lab loomed like the gate to hell, and Gillian had trouble keeping Thoughtful pinned to her face. But she managed to walk through it and into the quiet buzz that was a class before a bell was about to ring.

(Okay, kid. Go up front and tell Mr. Wizard you need a new book. He'll take care of the rest.)

Gillian did as Angel said. As she stood beside Mr. Leveret and told her story she sensed a new quietness in the classroom behind her. She didn't look back and she didn't raise her voice. By the time she was done, Mr. Leveret's pouchy, pleasantly ugly face had gone from a startled "Who are you?" expression (he had to look in the class register to make sure of her name) to one of pained sympathy.

"I've got an extra textbook," he said. "And some outlines of my lectures on transparencies. But as for notes—"

He turned to the class at large. "Okay, people. Jill—uh,

Gillian—needs a little help. She needs somebody who's willing to share their notes, maybe xerox them—"

Before he could finish his sentence, hands went up all over the room.

Somehow that brought everything into focus for Gillian. She was standing in front of a classroom with everyone staring at her—that in itself would have been enough to terrify her in the old days. And sitting there in front was David, wearing an unreadable expression, and Tanya, looking rigidly shocked. And other people who'd never looked directly at her before, and who were now waving their hands enthusiastically.

All boys.

She recognized Bruce Faber, who she'd always thought of as Bruce the Athlete, with his tawny hair and his blue-gray eyes and his tall football build. Normally he looked as if he were acknowledging the applause of a crowd. Just now he looked as if he were graciously extending an invitation to Gillian.

And Macon Kingsley, who she called Macon the Wallet because he was so rich. His hair was brown and styled, his eyes hooded, and there was something cruel to the sensual droop of his mouth. But he wore a Rolex and had a new sports car and right now he was looking at Gillian as if he'd pay a lot of money for her.

And Cory Zablinski—who was Cory the Party Guy because he constantly seemed to be arranging, going to, or just recovering from parties. Cory was wiry and hyper, with foxy

brown hair and darting fox-colored eyes. He had more personality than looks, but he was always in the middle of things, and
at this moment he was waving madly at Gillian.

Even Amy's new boyfriend Eugene, who didn't have looks
or personality in Gillian's opinion, was wiggling his fingers
eagerly.

David had his hand up, too, despite Tanya's cold expression. He looked polite and stubborn. Gillian wondered if he'd
told Tanya he was just trying to help a poor junior out.

(Pick . . . Macon.) The ghostly voice in Gillian's ear was
thoughtful.

(Macon? I thought maybe Cory.) She couldn't pick David,
of course, not with Tanya looking daggers at her. And she felt
uncomfortable about picking Bruce for the same reason—
his girlfriend Amanda Spengler was sitting right beside him.
Cory was friendly and, well, accessible. Macon, on the other
hand, was vaguely creepy.

This time the voice in her head was patient. (Have I ever
steered you wrong? Macon.)

(Cory's the one who always knows about parties. . . .) But
Gillian was already moving toward Macon. The most impor-
tant thing in life, she was discovering quickly, was to trust
Angel absolutely.

"Thanks," she said softly to Macon as she perched on an
empty stool behind him. She repeated after Angel: "I'll bet you
take good notes. You seem like a good observer."

Macon the Wallet barely inclined his head. She noticed that his hooded eyes were moss green, an unusual, almost disturbing color.

But he was nice to her all period. He promised to have his father's secretary photocopy the thick sheaf of biology notes in his spiral-bound notebook. He lent her a highlighter. And he kept looking at her as if she were some interesting piece of art.

That wasn't all. Cory the Party Guy dropped a ball of paper on the lab table as he walked past to get rid of his gum in the trash can. When Gillian unfolded it she found a Hershey's kiss and a questionnaire: *R U new? Do U like music? What's yr phone #?* And Bruce the Athlete tried to catch her eye whenever she glanced in his direction.

A warm and heady glow was starting somewhere inside Gillian.

But the most amazing part was yet to come. Mr. Leveret, pacing in the front, asked for somebody to review the five kingdoms used to categorize living things.

(Raise your hand, kid.)

(But I don't remember—)

(Trust me.)

Gillian's hand went up. The warm feeling had changed to a sense of dread. She *never* answered questions in class. She almost hoped Mr. Leveret wouldn't see her, but he spotted her right away and nodded.

"Gillian?"

(Now just say after me . . .) The soft voice in her head went on.

"Okay, the five classes would be, from most advanced to most primitive, Animalia, Plantae, Fungi, Protista, . . . and Eugene." Gillian ticked them off on her fingers and glanced sideways at Eugene as she finished.

(But that's not *nice*. I mean—)

She never got to what she meant. The entire class was roaring with laughter. Even Mr. Leveret rolled his eyes at the ceiling and shook his head tolerantly.

They thought she was hysterical. Witty. One of those types who could break up a whole classroom.

(But Eugene—)

(Look at him.)

Eugene was blushing pink, ducking his head. Grinning. He didn't look embarrassed or hurt; he actually looked pleased at the attention.

It's still wrong, a tiny voice that wasn't Angel's seemed to whisper. But it was drowned out by the laughter and the rising warmth inside Gillian. She'd never felt so accepted, so *included*. She had the feeling that now people would laugh whenever she said something even marginally funny. Because they *wanted* to laugh; they wanted to be pleased by her—and to please her.

(Rule One, dragonfly. A beautiful girl can tease any guy

and make him like it. No matter what the joke is. Am I right or am I right?)

(Angel, you're always right.) She meant it with all her heart. She had never imagined that guardian angels could be like this, but she was glad beyond words that they were and that she had one on her side.

At break the miracles continued. Instead of hurrying out the door as she normally did, she found herself walking slowly and lingering in the hall. She couldn't help it, both Macon and Cory were in front of her, talking to her.

"I can have the notes ready for you this weekend," Macon the Wallet was saying. "Maybe I should drop them by your house." His heavy-lidded eyes seemed to bore into her and the sensual droop to his mouth became more pronounced.

"No, I've got a better idea," Cory was saying, almost dancing around the two of them. "Mac, m'man, don't you think it's about time you had another party? I mean, it's been weeks, and you've got that big house. . . . How about Saturday, and I'll round up a keg and we can all get to know Jill better." He gestured expansively.

"Good idea," Bruce the Athlete said cheerfully from behind Gillian. "I'm free Saturday. What about you—Jill?" He draped a casual arm around her shoulder.

"Ask me Friday," Gillian said with a smile, repeating the whispered words in her mind. She shrugged off the arm on her own volition. Bruce belonged to Amanda.

A party for me, Gillian thought dazedly. All she'd wanted was to get *invited* to a party given by these kids—she'd never imagined being the focus of one. She felt a stinging in her nose and eyes and a sort of desperation in her stomach. Things were happening almost too fast.

Other people were gathering around curiously. Incredibly, she was at the center of a crowd and everyone seemed to be either talking to her or about her.

"Hey, are you new?"

"That's Gillian Lennox. She's been here for years."

"I never saw her before."

"You just never *noticed* her before."

"Hey, Jill, how come you lost your biology book?"

"Didn't you hear? She fell in a creek trying to save some kid. Almost drowned."

"I heard David Blackburn pulled her out and had to give her artificial respiration."

"*I* heard they were parked on Hillcrest Road this morning."

It was intoxicating, exhilarating. And it wasn't just guys who were gathered around her. She would have thought that the girls would be jealous, spiteful, that they'd glare at her or even all walk away from her in one mass snub.

But there was Kimberlee Cherry, Kim the Gymnast, the bubbly, sparkly little dynamo with her sun-blond curls and her baby-blue eyes. She was laughing and chattering. And there was Steffi Lockhart the Singer, with her café au lait skin and her soulful amber eyes, waving an expressive hand and beaming.

Even Amanda the Cheerleader, Bruce Faber's girlfriend, was in the group. She was flashing her healthy, wide smile and tossing her shiny brown hair, her fresh face glowing.

Gillian understood suddenly. The girls couldn't hate her, or couldn't show it if they did. Because Gillian had *status*, the instant and unassailable status that came from being beautiful and having guys fall all over themselves for her. She was a rising star, a force, a power to be reckoned with. And any girl who snubbed her was risking a nick in her own popularity if Gillian should decide to retaliate. They were *afraid* not to be nice to her.

It was dizzying, all right. Gillian felt as beautiful as an angel and as dangerous as a serpent. She was riding on waves of energy and adulation.

But then she saw something that made her feel as if she had suddenly stepped off a cliff.

Tanya had David by the arm and they were walking away down the hall.

CHAPTER 8

Gillian stood perfectly still and watched David disappear around a corner.

(It's not time for the plan yet, kid. Now buck up. A cheery face is worth diamonds.)

Gillian tried to put on a cheery face.

The strange day continued. In each class, Gillian appealed to the teacher for a new book. In each class, she was bombarded with offers of notes and other help. And through it all Angel whispered in her ear, always suggesting just the right thing to say to each person. He was witty, irreverent, occasionally cutting—and so was Gillian.

She had an advantage, she realized. Since nobody had ever noticed her before, it was almost like being a new girl. She could be anything she wanted to be, present herself as anyone, and be believed.

(Like Cinderella at the ball. The mystery princess.) Angel's voice was amused but tender.

In journalism class, Gillian found herself beside Daryl Novak, a languid girl with sloe eyes and drooping contemptuous lashes. Daryl the Rich Girl, Daryl the World-weary World Traveler. She talked to Gillian as if Gillian knew all about Paris and Rome and California.

At lunch, Gillian hesitated as she walked into the cafeteria. Usually she sat with Amy in an obscure corner at the back. But recently Eugene had been sitting with Amy, and up front she could see a group that included Amanda the Cheerleader, Kim the Gymnast, and others from The Clique. David and Tanya were at the edge.

(Do I sit with them? Nobody asked me.)

(Not with them, my little rutabaga. But near them. Sit at the end of that table just beside them. Don't look at them as you walk by. Look at your lunch. Start eating it.)

Gillian had never eaten her lunch alone before—or at least not in a public place. On days Amy was absent, if she couldn't find one of the few other juniors she felt comfortable with, she snuck into the library and ate there.

In the old days she would have felt horribly exposed, but now she wasn't really alone; she had Angel cracking jokes in her ear. And she had a new confidence. She could almost see herself eating, calm and indifferent to stares, thoughtful to the point of being dreamy. She tried to make her movements a little languid, like Daryl the Rich Girl's.

(And I hope Amy doesn't think I'm snubbing her. I mean, it's not as if she's back there alone. She's got Eugene.)

(Yeah. We're gonna have to talk about Amy sometime, kid. But right now you're being paged. Smile and be gracious.)

"Jill! Earth to Jill!"

"Hey, Jill, c'mon over."

They wanted her. She was moving her lunch over to their table, and she wasn't spilling anything and she wasn't falling as she slid in. She was little and graceful, thistledown light in her movements, and they were surging around her to form a warm and friendly bulwark.

And she wasn't afraid of them. That was the most wonderful thing of all. These kids who'd seemed to her like stars in some TV show about teenagers, were real people who got crumbs on themselves and made jokes she could understand.

Gillian had always wondered what they found so *funny* when they were laughing together. But now she knew it was just the heady atmosphere, the knowledge that they were special. It made it easy to laugh at everything. She knew David, sitting quietly there with Tanya, could see her laughing.

She could hear other voices occasionally, from people on the fringes of her group, people on the outside looking in. Mostly bright chatter and murmurs of admiration. She thought she heard her name mentioned. . . .

And then she focused on the words.

"I heard her mom's a drunk."

They sounded horribly loud and clear to Gillian, standing out against the background noise. She could feel her whole skin tingling with shock and she lost track of the story Kim the Gymnast was telling.

(Angel—who said that? Was it about me—my mom?) She didn't dare look behind her.

"—started drinking a few years ago and having these hallucinations—"

This time the voice was so loud that it cut through the banter of Gillian's group. Kim stopped in midsentence. Bruce the Athlete's smile faltered. An awkward silence fell.

Gillian felt a wave of anger that made her dizzy. (Who said that? I'll kill them—)

(Calm down! Calm *down*. That's not the way to handle it at all.)

(But—)

(I said, calm down. Look at your lunch. No, at your *lunch*. Now say—and make your voice absolutely cool—"I really hate rumors, don't you? I don't know what kind of people start them.")

Gillian breathed twice and obeyed, although her voice wasn't absolutely cool. It had a little tremor.

"I don't know either," a new voice said. Gillian glanced up to see that David was on his feet, his face hard as he surveyed the table behind her as if looking for the person who'd spoken.

"But I think they're pretty sick and they should get a life."

There was the cold glint in his eyes that had given him his reputation as a tough guy. Gillian felt as if a hand had steadied her. Gratitude rushed through her—and a longing that made her bite down on her lip.

"I hate rumors, too," J. Z. Oberlin said in her absent voice. J. Z. the Model was the one who looked like a Calvin Klein ad, breathlessly sexy and rather blank, but right now she seemed oddly focused. "Somebody was putting around the rumor last year that I tried to kill myself. I never did find out who started it." Her hazy blue-green eyes were narrowed.

And then everyone was talking about rumors, and people who spread rumors, and what scum they were. The group was rallying around Gillian.

But it was David who stood up for me first, she thought.

She had just looked over at him, trying to catch his eye, when she heard the tinkling noise.

It was almost musical, but the kind of sound that draws attention immediately in a cafeteria. Somebody had broken a glass. Gillian, along with everyone else, glanced around to see who'd done it.

She couldn't see anybody. No one had the right expression of dismay, no one was focused on anything definite. Everybody was looking around in search mode.

Then she heard it again, and two people standing near the cafeteria doors looked down and then up.

Above the doors, far above, was a semi-circular window in the red brick. As Gillian stared at the window she realized that light was reflecting off it oddly, almost prismatically. There seemed to be crazy rainbows in the glass. . . .

And something was sparkling down, falling like a few specks of snow. It hit the ground and tinkled, and the people by the door stared at it on the cafeteria floor. They looked puzzled.

Realization flashed on Gillian. She was on her feet, but the only words that she could find were, "Oh, my God!"

"Get out! It's all going to go! Get out of there!" It was David, waving at the people under the window. He was running toward them, which was *stupid*, Gillian thought numbly, her heart seeming to stop.

Other people were shouting. Cory and Amanda and Bruce—and Tanya. Kim the Gymnast was shrieking. And then the window *was* going, chunks of it falling almost poetically, raining and crumbling, shining and crashing. It fell and fell and fell. Gillian felt as if she were watching an avalanche in slow motion.

At last it was over, and the window was just an arch-shaped hole with jagged teeth clinging to the edges. Glass had flown and bounced and skittered all over the cafeteria, where it lay like hailstones. And people from tables amazingly distant were examining cuts from ricocheting bits.

But nobody had been directly underneath, and nobody seemed seriously hurt.

(Thanks to David.) Gillian was still numb, but now with relief. (He got them all out of the way in time. Oh, God, *he* isn't hurt, is he?)

(He's fine. And what makes you think he did it all alone? Maybe I had some part. I can do that, you know—put it into people's heads to do things. And they never even know I'm doing it.) Angel's voice sounded almost—well—piqued.

(Huh? You did that? Well, that was really nice of you.) Gillian was watching David across the room, watching Tanya examine his arm, nod, shrug, look around.

He's *not* hurt. Thank heaven. Gillian felt so relieved it was almost painful.

It was then that it occurred to her to wonder what had happened.

That window—before the glass fell it had looked just like the mirror in her bathroom. Evenly shattered from side to side, spidery cracks over every inch of the surface.

The bathroom mirror had cracked while Tanya was being catty about Gillian's room. *Now* Gillian remembered the last thing she'd wanted to ask Angel last night. It had been about how the mirror came to do that.

This window . . . it had started falling a few minutes after someone insulted Gillian's mother. Nobody had heard it actually break, but it couldn't have happened too long ago.

The small hairs on the back of Gillian's neck stirred and she felt a fluttering inside.

It couldn't be. Angel hadn't even appeared to her yet. . . .

But he'd said he was always with her. . . .

An angel wouldn't *destroy* things. . . .

But Angel was a different kind of angel.

(Ah, excuse me. Hello? Do you want to share some thoughts with me?)

(Angel!) For the first time since his soft voice had sounded in her ear, Gillian felt a sense of—overcrowdedness. Of her own lack of privacy. The uneasy fluttering inside her increased. (Angel, I was just—just wondering . . .) And then the silent words burst out. (Angel, you *wouldn't*—would you? You didn't do those things for my sake—break the mirror and that window—?)

A pause. And then, in her head, riotous laughter. *Genuine* laughter. Angel was whooping.

Finally, the sounds died to mental hiccups. *(Me?)*

Gillian was embarrassed. (I shouldn't have asked. It was just so weird. . . .)

(Yeah, wasn't it.) This time Angel sounded grimly amused. (Well, never mind; you're already late for class. The bell rang five minutes ago.)

Gillian coasted through her last two classes in a daze. So much had happened today—she felt as if she'd led a full life between waking up and now.

But the day wasn't over yet.

In her last class, studio art, she once again found herself

talking to Daryl the Rich Girl. Daryl was the only one of that crowd that took art or journalism. And in the last minutes before school ended, she regarded Gillian from under drooping eyelashes.

"You know, there are other rumors going around about you. That you and Davey-boy have something going behind Tanya's back. That you meet secretly in the mornings and . . ." Daryl shrugged, pushing back frosted hair with a hand dripping with rings.

Gillian felt jolted awake. "So?"

"So you really should do something about it. Rumors spread fast, and they grow. I know. You want to either deny them, or"—Daryl's lips quirked in a smile—"disarm them."

(Oh, yeah? And just how do I do that?)

(Shut up and listen to her, kid. This is one smart cookie.)

"If there're parts that are true, it's usually best to admit those in public. That takes some of the punch out. And it's *always* helpful to track down the person starting the rumors—if you can."

(Tell her you know that. And that you're going to see Tanya after school.)

(*Tanya?* You mean—?)

(Just tell her.)

Somehow Gillian gathered herself enough to repeat Angel's words.

Daryl the Rich Girl looked at her with a new expression of

respect. "You're sharper than I thought. Maybe you didn't need my help after all."

"No," Gillian said without Angel's prompting. "I'm always glad for help. It's—it's a rough world."

"Isn't it, though?" Daryl said and raised already arched eyebrows.

(So it was Tanya who spread that stuff about my mom.) Gillian almost stumbled as she trudged out of art class. She was tired and bewildered. Somehow, she'd have thought Tanya was above that.

(She had help. It takes a really efficient system to get a rumor to peak circulation that fast. But she was the instigator. Turn left here.)

(Where am I going?)

(You're gonna catch her coming out of marketing education. She's alone in there right now. The teacher asked to see her after class, then unexpectedly had to run to the bathroom.)

Gillian felt distantly amused. She sensed Angel's hand in these arrangements.

And when she poked her head inside the marketing ed room, she saw that Tanya was indeed alone. The tall girl was standing by a cloudy green blackboard.

"Tanya, we need to talk."

Tanya's shoulders stiffened. Then she ran a hand across her already perfect dark hair and turned. She looked more like a future executive than ever, with her face set in cool lines and her exotic gray eyes running over Gillian in appraisal. Without Angel, Gillian would have dried up and withered away under that scrutiny.

Tanya said one word. "Talk."

What followed was more like a play than a conversation for Gillian. She repeated what Angel whispered to her, but she never had any idea what was coming. The only way to survive was to give herself up completely to his direction.

"Look, I know you're upset with me, Tanya. But I'd like to deal with this with a little maturity, okay?" She followed Angel's instructions over to a desk and brushed absent fingers over its imitation-wood top. "I don't think there's any need for us to act like children."

"And *I* don't think I know what you're talking about."

"Oh, really?" Gillian turned and looked Tanya in the face. "I think you know exactly what I'm talking about." (Angel, I feel just like one of those people in a soap opera—)

"Well, you're wrong. And, as a matter of fact, I happen to be busy—"

"I'm talking about the rumors, Tanya. I'm talking about the stories about my mom. And I'm talking about David."

Tanya stood perfectly still. For a moment she seemed surprised that Gillian was taking such a direct approach. Then her gray eyes hardened with the clear light of battle.

"All right, let's talk about David," she said in a pleasant voice, moving tigerishly toward Gillian. "I don't know about any rumors, but I'd like to hear what you and David were doing this morning. Care to tell me?"

(Angel, she's actually *enjoying* this. Look at her! And she's *bigger* than me.)

(Trust me, kid.)

"We weren't doing anything," Gillian said. She had to tip her chin up to look Tanya in the face. Then she looked aside and shook her head. "All right. I'll be honest about that. I like David, Tanya. I have ever since he moved in. He's good and he's noble and he's honest and he's sweet. But that doesn't mean I want to take him away from you. In fact, it's just the opposite."

She turned and walked away, looking into the distance. "I think David deserves the best. And I know he really cares about you. And *that's* what happened this morning—he told me you guys had made a promise to each other. So you see, you've got no reason to be suspicious."

Tanya's eyes were glittering. "Don't try to pull that. All this . . ." She waved a hand to indicate Gillian's dress and hair. "In one day you turn from Little Miss Invisible to *this*. And you start prancing around the school like you own it. You can't pretend you're not trying to get him."

"Tanya, the way I dress has nothing at all to do with David." Gillian told the lie calmly, facing the chalk-misted blackboard again. "It's just—something I needed to do. I was—tired of being invisible," She turned her head slightly, not enough to see Tanya. "But that's beside the point. The real issue here is what's best for David. And I think *you're* best for him—as long as you treat him fairly."

"And what is *that* supposed to mean?" Tanya was losing her legendary cool. She sounded venomous, almost shrill.

"It means no more fooling around with Bruce Faber." (*Oh, my God,* Angel! Bruce Faber? Bruce the Athlete? She's been fooling around with *Bruce Faber?*)

Tanya's voice cracked like a whip. "What are you talking about? What do you know?"

"I'm talking about those nights at the pool parties last summer in Macon's cabana. While David was up north at his grandma's. I'm talking about what happened in Bruce's car after the Halloween dance." (In a *cabana?*)

There was a silence. When Tanya spoke again, her voice was a sort of icy explosion. "How did you find out?"

Gillian shrugged. "People who're good at spreading rumors can be a two-edged sword."

"I thought so. That *brat* Kim! Her and her mouth . . ." Then Tanya's voice changed. It became a voice with claws and Gillian could tell she was moving closer. "I suppose you're planning to tell David about this?"

"Huh?" For a moment Gillian was too confused to follow Angel's directions. Then she got hold of herself. "Oh, of course I'm not going to tell David. That's why I'm telling *you.* I just want you to promise that you're not going to do anything like that anymore. And I'd appreciate it if you'd stop telling people things about my mom—"

"I'll do worse than that!" Suddenly Tanya was standing right behind Gillian. Her voice was a yelling hiss. "You have no *idea* what I'll do if you try to mess with me, you snotty little midget. You are going to be so sorry—"

"No, I think you've done plenty already."

The voice came from the door. Gillian heard it, and in that instant she understood everything.

CHAPTER 9

It was David, of course.

Gillian turned around and stared at him, blinking. He was standing just inside the doorway, his jacket slung over one shoulder, the other hand in his pocket. His jaw was tight, his eyes dark. He was looking at Tanya.

There was a silence.

(How long? How long has he been there, Angel?)

(Uhhh, I'd say since round about . . . the beginning.)

(Oh, my.) So that's why Gillian had been so low-key and noble and let Tanya do all the yelling and threatening. They must have come off like Dorothy and the Wicked Witch.

A sense of justice stirred inside Gillian. She made a hesitant move toward David.

"David—you don't understand—"

David shook his head. "I understand just fine. Don't try to cover for her. It's better for me to find out."

(Yeah, shut up, minibrain! Now look mildly distressed, slightly awkward. You guess they want to be alone now.)

"Uh, I guess you guys want to be alone now."

(Anyway, you have to hurry to get your ride.)

"Anyway, I have to hurry to get my ride."

(These aren't the droids you're looking for.)

"These aren't—" (I'm going to *kill* you, Angel!) Flustered, Gillian made one last gesture of apology and almost ran for the door.

Outside, she walked blindly. (Angel!)

(Sorry, I couldn't resist. But look at you, kid! Do you know what you've done?)

(I guess . . . I got rid of Tanya.) As the adrenaline of battle faded, the truth of this was slowly beginning to dawn on her. It brought a hint of glorious warmth, a sparkling promise of future happiness.

(Smart kid!)

(And—I did it fairly. It *was* all true, wasn't it, Angel? She's really been messing around with Bruce?)

(Everybody's been messing around with Bruce. Yes, it was all true.)

(And what about Kim? Is she the one who spreads rumors about people?)

(Like butter on Eggos.)

(I just—she seemed so *sweet*. When we talked about rumors in the cafeteria she patted my hand.)

(Sure, she's sweet—to your face. Turn left here.)

Gillian found herself emerging from the school building. As she went down the steps she saw three or four cars parked casually in the roundabout. Macon's BMW convertible was one. He looked up at her and gave an inviting nod toward the car.

Other people shouted. "Hey, Jill, need a ride?" "We wouldn't want you to get lost in the woods again!"

Gillian stood, feeling like a southern belle. So many people wanting her—it made her giddy. Angel was grandly indifferent (Pick anybody!) and she could see Amy's Geo a little distance away. Amy and Eugene were standing by it, looking up at her. But getting in a car with Eugene Elfred would be disastrous to her new status.

She picked Cory the Party Guy, and the ride home was filled with his nonstop talk about Macon's party on Saturday. She had trouble getting rid of him at the door. Once she did, she walked up to her bedroom and fell on her bed, arms out. She stared at the ceiling.

(Phew!)

It had been the most incredible day of her life.

She lay and listened to the quiet house and tried to gather her thoughts.

The warmth was still percolating inside her, although it was mixed with a certain amount of anxiety. She wanted to see David again. She wanted to know how things had turned out with Tanya. She couldn't let herself feel happy until she was sure . . .

"Relax, would you?"

Gillian sat up. The voice wasn't in her ear, it was beside the bed. Angel was sitting there.

The sight hit her like a physical blow.

She hadn't seen him since that morning and she'd forgotten how beautiful he was.

His hair was dark golden with paler gold lights shimmering in it. His face was—well—classic perfection. Absolutely pure, defined like a sculpture in marble. His eyes were a violet so glorious it actually hurt to look at it. His expression was rapt and uplifted . . . until he winked. Then it dissolved into mischief.

"Uh, hi," Gillian whispered huskily.

"Hi, kid. Tired?"

"Yeah. I feel . . . used up."

"Well, take a nap, why don't you? I've got places to go anyway."

Gillian blinked. Places? "Angel . . . I never asked you. What's heaven like? I mean, with angels like you, it's got to be different from most people's idea. That meadow I saw—that wasn't it, was it?"

"No, that wasn't it. Heaven—well, it's hard to explain. It's all in the oscillation of the spatial-temporal harmonics, you know—what you'd call the inherent vibration of the plane. At a higher vibration everything assumes a much more complicated harmonic theme. . . ."

"You're making this up, aren't you?"

"Yeah. Actually it's classified. Why don't you get some sleep?"

Gillian already had her eyes shut.

She was happy when she woke up to smell dinner. But when she got downstairs, she found only her mother.

"Dad's not home?"

"No. He called, honey, and left a message for you. He'll be out of town on business for a while."

"But he'll be back for Christmas. Won't he?"

"I'm sure he will."

Gillian didn't say anything else. She ate the hamburger casserole her mother served—and noticed that her mother didn't eat. Afterward, she sat in the kitchen and played with a fork.

(You okay?)

The voice in her ear was a welcome relief. (Angel. Yeah, I'm all right. I was just thinking . . . about how everything started with Mom. It wasn't always like this. She was a teacher at the junior college. . . .)

(I know.)

(And then—I think it was about five years ago—things just started happening. She started acting crazy. And then she was seeing things—what did I know about drinking then? I just thought she was nuts. It wasn't until Dad started finding empty bottles . . .)

(I know.)

(I just wish . . . that things could be different.) A pause. (Angel? Do you think maybe they could be?)

Another pause. Then Angel's voice was quiet. (I'll work on it, kid. But, yeah, I think maybe they could be.)

Gillian shut her eyes.

After a moment she opened them again. (Angel—how can I thank you? The things you're doing for me . . . I can't even start to tell you . . .)

(Don't mention it. And don't cry. A cheery face is worth triple A bonds. Besides, you have to answer the phone.)

(What phone?)

The phone rang.

(That phone.)

Gillian blew her nose and said a practice "Hello" to make sure her voice wasn't shaky. Then she took a deep breath and picked up the receiver.

"Gillian?"

Her fingers clenched on the phone. "Hi, David."

"Look, I just wanted to make sure you were okay. I didn't even ask you that when—you know, this afternoon."

"Sure, I'm okay." Gillian didn't need Angel to tell her what to say to this. "I can handle myself, you know."

"Yeah. But Tanya can be pretty intense sometimes. After you left she was—well, forget that."

He doesn't want to say anything bad about her, Gillian thought. She said, "I'm fine."

"It's just—" She could almost feel the frustration building on the other side of the line. And then David burst out as if something had snapped, "I didn't know!"

"What?"

"I didn't know she was—like that! I mean, she runs the teen helpline and she's on the Centralia relief committee and the Food Cupboard project and . . . Anyway, I thought she was different. A good person."

Conscience twinged. "David, I think she *is* some of the things you thought. She's brave. When that window—"

"Quit it, Gillian. *You're* those things. *You're* brave and funny and—well, too honorable for your own good. You tried to give Tanya another chance." He let out a breath. "But, anyway; you might have guessed, we're finished. I told Tanya that. And now . . ." His voice changed. Suddenly he laughed, sounding as if some burden had fallen off him. "Well, would you like me to drive you to the party Saturday night?"

Gillian laughed, too. "I'd like it. I'd love it." (Oh, Angel— *thank you!*)

She was very happy.

The rest of the week was wonderful. Every day she wore something daring and flattering scavenged from the depths of her closet. Every day she seemed to get more popular. People looked up when she walked into a room, not just meeting her eyes, but trying to catch her eye. They waved to her from a distance. They said hello up and down the halls. Everyone seemed glad to talk to her, and pleased if she wanted to talk to them. It was like being on a skyrocket, going higher and higher.

And, always, her guide and protector was with her. Angel had come to seem like a part of her, the most savvy and ingenious part. He provided quips, smoothed over awkward situations, gave advice about who to tolerate and who to snub. Gillian was developing an instinct for this, too. She was gaining confidence in herself, finding new skills every day. She was literally becoming a new person.

She didn't see much of Amy now. But Amy had Eugene, after all. And Gillian was so busy that she never even got to see David alone.

The day of the party she went to Houghton with Amanda the Cheerleader and Steffi the Singer. They laughed a lot, got whistled at everywhere, and shopped until they were dizzy. Gillian bought a dress and ankle boots—both approved by Angel.

When David picked her up that night, he let out a soft whistle himself.

"I look okay?"

"You look . . ." He shook his head. "Illegal, but also sort of spiritual. How do you *do* that?"

Gillian smiled.

Macon the Wallet's house was the house of a rich guy. A fleet of artsy reindeer made out of some kind of white twigs and glowing with tiny lights graced the lawn. Inside, it was all high ceilings and track lighting, oriental rugs, old china, silver. Gillian was dazzled.

(My first *real* party! I mean, my first Popular Party. And it's even kind of, sort of for *me*.)

(Your first real party, and it's all for you. The world is your oyster, kid. Go out and crack it.)

Macon was coming toward her. Other people were looking. Gillian paused in the doorway of the room for effect, aware that she was making an entrance—and loving it.

Her outfit was designer casual. A black minidress with a pattern of purple flowers so dark it could hardly be distinguished. The soft, crepey material clung to her like a second skin. Matte black tights. And of course the ankle boots. Not much makeup; she'd decided on the fresh, soft look for her face. She'd darkened her lashes just enough to make the violet of her eyes a startling contrast.

She looked stunning . . . and effortless. And she knew it very well.

Macon's hooded eyes roved over her with something like suppressed hunger. "How's it going? You're looking good."

"We feel good," Gillian said, squeezing David's arm.

Macon's eyes darkened. He looked at the intersection of Gillian's hand and David's arm as if it offended him.

David looked back dispassionately, but a sort of wordless menace exuded from him. Macon actually took a step back.

But all he said was, "Well, my parents are gone for the weekend, so make yourself at home. There should be food somewhere."

There was food everywhere. Every kind of munchy thing. Music blasted from the den, echoing all over the house. As they walked in, Cory greeted them with, "Hey, guys! Grab a glass, it's going fast."

When he'd said that he would round up a keg last week, Gillian had foolishly misheard it as "a cake." Now she understood. It was a keg of beer and everybody was drinking.

And not just beer. There were hard liquor bottles around. One guy was lying on a table with his mouth open while a girl poured something from a rectangular bottle into it.

"Hey, Jill, this is for you." Cory was trying to give her a plastic glass with foam overflowing the top.

Gillian looked at him with open scorn. She didn't need Angel's help for this.

"Thanks, but I happen to *like* my brain cells. Maybe if you had more respect for yours you wouldn't be flunking biology."

There was laughter. Even Cory laughed and winced.

"Right on," Daryl the Rich Girl said, raising a can of diet Barq's root beer to Gillian in salute. And David waved Cory away and reached for a Coke.

Nobody tried to pressure them and the guy on the table even looked a little embarrassed. Gillian had learned that you could pull anything off if you were cool enough, composed enough, and if you didn't back down. The feeling of success was much more intoxicating than liquor could have been.

(How about that? Pretty good, huh? Huh? Huh?)

(Oh . . . oh, yeah, fine.) Angel seemed to deliberate. (Of course, it does say, "Wine maketh the heart of man glad. . . .")

(Oh, Angel, you're so silly. You sound like Cory!) Gillian almost laughed out loud.

Everything was exciting. The music, the huge house with its opulent Christmas decorations. The people. All the girls threw their arms around Gillian and kissed her as if they hadn't seen her in weeks. Some of the boys tried, but David warned them off with a look.

That was exciting, too. Having everyone know she was together with David Blackburn, that he was *hers.* It put her status through the ceiling.

"Want to look around?" David was saying. "I can show you the upstairs; Macon doesn't care."

Gillian looked at him. "Bored?"

He grinned. "No. But I wouldn't mind seeing you alone for a few minutes."

They went up a long carpeted staircase lined with oil paintings. The rooms upstairs were just as beautiful as downstairs: palatial and almost awe inspiring.

It put Gillian in a quiet mood. The music wasn't as loud up here, and the cool marble gave her the feeling of being in a museum.

She looked out a window to see velvet darkness punctuated by little twinkling lights.

"You know, I'm glad you didn't want to drink back there." David's voice behind her was quiet.

She turned, trying to read his face. "But . . . you were surprised?"

"Well—it's just sometimes now you seem *so* adult. Sort of worldly."

"Me? I mean—I mean *you're* the one who seems like that." And that's what you like in girls, she thought.

He looked away and laughed. "Oh, yeah. The tough guy. The wild guy. Tanya and I used to party pretty hard." He shrugged. "I'm not tough. I'm just a small-town guy trying to get through life. I don't look for trouble. I try to run from it if I can."

Gillian had to laugh herself at that. But there was something serious in David's dark eyes.

"I admit, it sort of had a way of finding me in the past," he said slowly. "And I've done some things that I'm not proud of. But, you know . . . I'd like to change that—if it's possible."

"Sort of like a whole new side of you that wants to come out."

He looked startled. Then he glanced up and down her and grinned. "Yeah. Sort of like that."

Gillian felt suddenly inspired, hopeful. "I think," she said slowly, trying to put her ideas together, "that sometimes people need to—to express both sides of themselves. And then they can be . . . well, whole."

"Yeah. If that's possible." He hesitated. Gillian didn't say anything, because she had the feeling that he was trying to. That there was some reason he'd brought her up to talk to her alone.

"Well. You know something weird?" he said after a moment. "I *don't* feel exactly whole. And the truth is—" He looked around the darkened room. Gillian could only see his profile. He shook his head, then took a deep breath. "Okay, this is going to sound even dumber than I thought, but I've got to say it. I can't help it."

He turned back toward her and said with a mixture of determination and apology, "And since that day when I found you out there in the snow, I have this feeling that I won't be, without . . ." He trailed off and shrugged. "Well—you," he said finally, helplessly.

The universe was one enormous heartbeat. Gillian could feel her body echoing it. She said slowly, "I . . ."

"I know. I *know* how it sounds. I'm sorry."

"No," Gillian whispered. "That wasn't what I was going to say."

He'd turned sharply away to glare at the window. Now he turned halfway back and she saw the glimmer of hope in his face.

"I was going to say, I understand."

He looked as if he were afraid to believe. "Yeah, but do you *really*?"

"I think I do—really."

And then he was moving toward her and Gillian was holding up her arms. Literally as if drawn to do it—but not just by physical attraction. It sounded crazy, Gillian thought, but it wasn't physical so much as . . . well, spiritual. They seemed to *belong* together.

David was holding her. It felt incredibly strange and at the same time perfectly natural. He was warm and solid and Gillian felt her eyes shutting, her head drifting to his shoulder. Such a simple embrace, but it seemed to mean everything.

The feelings inside Gillian were like a wonderful discovery. And she had the sense that she was on the verge of some other discovery, that if she just opened her eyes and looked into David's at this moment, somehow it would mean a change in the world. . . .

(Kid?) The voice in Gillian's ear was quiet. (I *really* hate to say it, but I have to break this up. You have to sidle down to the master bedroom.)

Gillian scarcely heard and couldn't pay attention.

(Gillian! I mean it, kid. There's something going on that you have to know about.)

(Angel?)

(Tell him you'll be back in a few minutes. This is important!)

There was no way to ignore that tone of urgency. Gillian

stirred. "David, I have to go for a sec. Be right back."

David just nodded. "Sure." It was Gillian who had trouble letting go of his hand, and when she did she still seemed to feel his grip.

(This had better be good, Angel.) She blinked in the light of the hallway.

(Go down to the end of the hall. That's the master bedroom. Go on in. Don't turn on the light.)

The master bedroom was cavernous and dark and filled with large dim shapes like sleeping elephants. Gillian walked in and immediately banged into a piece of heavy furniture.

(Be careful! See that light over there?)

Light was showing around the edges of double doors on the other side of the room. The doors were closed.

(And locked. That's the bathroom. Now, here's what I want you to do. Walk carefully over to the right of the bathroom and you'll find another door. It's the closet. I want you to quietly open that door and get in it.)

(What?)

Angel's voice was elaborately patient. (Get in the closet and put your ear against the wall.)

Gillian shut her eyes. Then, feeling exactly like a burglar, she slowly turned the handle of the closet door and slipped inside.

It was a walk-in closet, very long but stuffy because of the clothes bristling from both sides. Gillian had a profound feeling of intrusion, of being an invader of privacy. She seemed to walk a long way in before Angel stopped her.

(Okay. Here. Now put your ear against the left wall.)

Eyes still shut—it seemed to make the absolute darkness more bearable—Gillian burrowed between something long sheathed in plastic and something heavy and velvety. With the clothes embracing her on either side, she leaned her head until her bare ear touched wood.

(Angel, I can't believe I'm doing this. I feel really stupid, and I'm scared, and if anybody finds me—)

(Just *listen*, will you?)

At first Gillian's heart seemed to drown out all other sounds. But then, faint but clear, she heard two voices she recognized.

CHAPTER 10

But only if you absolutely *swear* to me you didn't do it."

"Oh, how many times? I've been telling you all week I didn't. I never said a *word* to her. I swear."

The first voice, which sounded taut and a little unbalanced, was Tanya's. The second was Kim the Gymnast's. Despite her brave words, Kim sounded scared.

(Angel? What's going on?)

(Trouble.)

"Okay," Tanya's voice was saying. "Then this is your chance to prove it by helping me."

"Tan, look. Look. I'm sorry about you and David breaking up. But maybe it's not Gillian's fault—"

"It's *completely* her fault. The stuff with Bruce was over. You know that. There was no reason for David to ever find out—until *she* opened her mouth. And as for how she found out—"

"Not again!" Kim the Gymnast sounded ready to scream. *"I didn't do it."*

"All right. I believe you." Tanya's voice was calmer. "So in that case there's no reason for us to fight. We've got to stick together. Hand me that brush, will you?" There was silence for a moment, and Gillian could imagine Tanya brushing her dark hair to a higher gloss, looking in a mirror approvingly.

"So what are you going to do?" Kim's voice asked.

"Get both of them. In a way, I hate him more. I promised he'd be sorry if he dumped me, and I always keep my promises."

Squashed between the heavy, swaying clothes on her right and left, Gillian had a wild and almost fatal impulse to giggle.

She knew what was going on. It was just such a . . . a *sitcom* situation that she had a hard time making herself believe in it. Here she was, listening to two people who were actually *plotting against her.* She was overhearing their plans to get her. It was . . . absurd. Bad mystery novel stuff.

And it was happening anyway.

She made a feeble attempt to get back to reality, straightening up slightly.

(Angel—people don't really do these revenge things. Right? They're just talking. And—I mean, I can't even believe I'm hearing all this. It's so . . . so *ridiculous* . . .)

(You're overhearing it because I brought you here. You have an invisible friend who can lead you to the right place at the right time. And you'd better believe that people carry out these "revenge things." Tanya's never made a plan that she hasn't carried through.)

(The future executive.) Gillian thought it faintly.

(Future CEO. She's deadly serious, kid. And she's smart. She can make things happen.)

Gillian no longer felt like giggling.

When she pressed her ear against the wall again, it was clear she'd missed some of the conversation.

". . . David first?" Kim the Gymnast was saying.

"Because I know what to do with him. He wants to get into Ohio University, you know? He sent the application in October. It was already going to be a little hard because his grades aren't great, but he scored really high on the SATs. It was hard, but I'm going to make it . . ." There was a pause and Tanya's voice seemed to mellow and sweeten. "Absolutely impossible."

"How?" Kim sounded shaken.

"By writing to the university. And to our principal and to Ms. Renquist, the English lit teacher, and to David's grandpa, who's supposed to be giving him money to go to college."

"But why? I mean, if you say something nasty, they'll just think it's sour grapes—"

"I'm going to tell them he passed English lit last year by cheating. We had to turn in a term paper. But he didn't write the paper he turned in. It was *bought*. From a college guy in Philadelphia."

Kim's breath whooshed out so loudly that Gillian could hear it. "How do you know?"

"Because I arranged it, of course. I wanted him to bring his grades up, to get into a university. To *make* something of himself. But of course he can never prove all that. He's the one that paid for it."

A silence. Then Kim said, with what sounded like forced lightness, "But, Tan, you could ruin his whole life. . . ."

"I know." Tanya's voice was serene. Satisfied.

"But . . . well, what do you want *me* to do?"

"Be ready to spread the word. That's what you do best, isn't it? I'll get the letters written by Monday. And then on Monday you can start telling people—because I want *everyone* to know. Prime that grapevine!" Tanya was laughing.

"Okay. Sure. Consider it done." Kim sounded more scared than ever. "Uh, look, I'd better get back downstairs now—can I use the brush a second?"

"Here." A clatter. "And, Kim? Be ready to help me with Gillian, too. I'll let you know what I've got in mind for her."

Kim said, "Sure,"—faintly. Then there were a few more clatters and the sound of a door rattling open and shut. Then silence.

Gillian stood in the stuffy closet.

She felt physically sick. As if she'd found something loathsome and slimy and unclean writhing under her bed. Tanya was *crazy*—and evil. Gillian had just seen into a mind utterly twisted with hatred.

And smart. Angel had said it.

(Angel, what do I *do*? She really means it, doesn't she? She's going to *destroy* him. And there isn't anything I can do about it.)

(There may be something.)

(She's not going to listen to reason. I *know* she's not. Nobody's going to be able to talk her out of it. And threats aren't any good—)

(I said, there may be something you can do.)

Gillian came back to herself. (What?)

(It's a little complicated. And . . . well, the truth is, you may not *want* to do it, kid.)

(I would do anything for David.) Gillian's response was instant and absolute. Strange, how there were some things you were so sure of.

(Okay. Well, hold that thought. I'll explain everything when we get home—which we should do *fast*. But first I want you to get something from that bathroom.)

Gillian felt calm and alert, like a young soldier on her first mission in enemy territory. Angel had an idea. As long as she did exactly what Angel said, things were going to turn out all right.

She went into the bathroom and followed Angel's instructions precisely without asking why. Then she went to get David to take her home from the party.

"I'm ready. Now tell me what I can do."

Gillian was sitting on her bed, wearing the pajamas with little bears on them. It was well after midnight and the house was quiet and dark except for the lamp on her nightstand.

"You know, I think you *are* ready."

The voice was quiet and thoughtful—and outside her head. In the air about two feet away from the bed, a light began to grow.

And then it was Angel, sitting lotus style, with his hands on his knees. Floating lotus style. He was about level with Gillian's bed and he was looking at her searchingly. His face was earnest and calm, and all around him was a pale, changing light like the aurora borealis.

As always, Gillian felt a physical reaction at the first sight of him. A sort of shock. He was so beautiful, so unearthly, so unlike anyone else.

And right now his eyes were more intense than she had ever seen them.

It scared her a little, but she pushed that—and the physical reaction—away. She had to think of David. David, who'd so trustingly taken her home when she "got sick" an hour ago, and who right now had absolutely no idea what was in store for him on Monday.

"Just tell me what to do," she said to Angel.

She was braced. She had no idea what it would take to stop Tanya, but it couldn't be anything pleasant—or legal. Didn't matter. She was ready.

So Angel's words were something of a letdown.

"You know you're special, don't you?"

"Huh?"

"You've always been special. And underneath, you've always known it."

Gillian wasn't sure what to say. Because it sounded terribly cliché—but it was true. She *was* special. She'd had a near-death experience. She'd come back with an angel. Surely only special people did that. And her popularity at school—everyone there certainly thought she was special. But her own inner feeling had started long before that, sometime in childhood. She'd just imagined that everybody felt that way . . . that they were different from others, maybe better, but certainly *different*.

"Well, everybody *does* feel that way, actually," Angel said, and Gillian felt a little jolt. She always felt it when she suddenly remembered her thoughts weren't private anymore.

Angel was going on. "But for you it happens to be true. Listen, what do you know about your great-grandma Elspeth?"

"*What?*" Gillian was lost. "She's an old lady. And, um, she lives in England and always sends me Christmas presents. . . ." She had a vague memory of a photograph showing a woman with white hair and white glasses, a tweed skirt and sensible shoes. The woman held a Pekingese in a little red jacket.

"She grew up in England, but she was born American. She was only a year old when she was separated from her big sister Edgith, who was raising her. It happened during World War One. Everyone thought she had no family, so she was given to an English couple to raise."

"Oh, really? How interesting." Gillian was not only bewildered but exasperated. "But what on *earth*—"

"Here's what it's got to do with David. Your great-grandma didn't grow up with her real sister, with her real family. If she had, she'd have known her real heritage. She'd have known . . ."

"Yes?"

"That she was born a witch."

There was a long, long silence. It shouldn't have been so long. After the first second Gillian thought of things to say, but somehow she couldn't get them past the tightness of her throat.

She ought to laugh. That was *funny*, the idea of Great-Grandma, with her sensible shoes, being a witch. And besides, witches didn't exist. They were just *stories*—

—like angels—

—or examples of New Age grown-ups acting silly.

"Angels," Gillian gasped in a strangled voice. She was beginning to feel wild inside. As if rules were breaking loose.

Because angels were true. She was looking at one. He was floating about two and a half feet off the floor. There was absolutely nothing under him and he could hear her thoughts and disappear and he was *real.* And if angels could be real . . .

Magic happens. She'd seen that on a bumper sticker somewhere. Now she clapped both hands to her mouth. There was something boiling up inside her and she wasn't sure if it was a scream or a giggle.

"My great-grandma is a *witch*?"

"Well, not exactly. She would be if she knew about her family. That's the key, you see—you have to know. Your great-grandma has the blood, and so does your grandma, and so does your mom. And so do you, Gillian. And now . . . you know." The last words were very gentle, very deliberate. As if Angel were delicately putting into place the last piece of a puzzle.

Gillian's laughter had faded. She felt dizzy, as if she had unexpectedly come to the edge of a cliff and looked over. "I'm . . . I've got the blood, too."

"Don't be afraid to say it. You're a witch."

"Angel . . ." Gillian's heart was beating very hard suddenly. Hard and slow. "Please . . . I don't really understand any of this. And . . . well, I'm *not*."

"A witch? You don't know how to be, yet. But as a matter of fact, kid, you're already showing the signs. Do you remember when that mirror broke in the downstairs bathroom?"

"I'm—"

"And when the window broke in the cafeteria. You asked me if *I* did those things. I didn't. You did. You were angry and you lashed out with your power . . . but you didn't realize it."

"Oh, God," Gillian whispered.

"It's a frightening thing, that power. When you don't know how to use it, it can cause all kinds of damage. To other people—and to you. Oh, kid, don't you understand? Look at what's happened to your mother."

"What about my mother?"

"She . . . is . . . a . . . witch. A lost witch, like you. She's got powers, but she doesn't know how to channel them, she doesn't understand them, and they terrify her. When she started seeing visions—"

"Visions!" Gillian sat straight up. It was as if a light had suddenly gone on in her head, illuminating five years of her life.

"Yeah." Angel's violet eyes were steady, his face grim. "The hallucinations came before the drinking, not after. And they were psychic visions, images of things that were going to happen, or that might have happened, or that happened a long time ago. But of course she didn't understand that."

"Oh, God. Oh, my God." Electricity was running up and down Gillian's body, setting her whole skin tingling. Tears stung in her eyes—not tears of sadness, but of pure, shocking revelation. "That's it. That's it. Oh, God, we've got to *help* her. We've got to *tell* her—"

"I agree. But first we have to get *you* under control. And it's not exactly a thing you can just spring on her without any warning. You could do more harm than good that way. We've got to build up to it."

"Yes. Yes, I see that. You're right." Gillian blinked rapidly. She tried to calm her breathing, to *think*.

"And just at the moment, she's stable. A little depressed, but stable. She'll wait until after Monday. But Tanya won't."

"Tanya?" Gillian had nearly forgotten the original discussion. "Oh, yeah, Tanya. Tanya." *David,* she thought.

"There is something very practical you can do about Tanya—now that you know what you are."

"Yes. All right." Gillian wet her lips. "Do you think Dad will come back if Mom realizes what she is and gets it all together?"

"I think there's a good possibility. But *listen* to me. To take care of Tanya—"

"Angel." A slow coil of anxiety was unrolling in Gillian's stomach. "Now that I think about it . . . I mean, aren't witches *bad*? Shouldn't you—well, *disapprove* of this?"

Angel put his golden head in his hands. "If I thought it was bad would I be here guiding you through it?"

Gillian almost laughed. It was so incongruous—the pale northern lights aura around him and the sound of him talking through clenched teeth.

Then a thought struck her. She spoke hesitantly and wonderingly. "Did you *come* here to guide me through it?"

He lifted his head and looked at her with those unearthly eyes. "What do you think?"

Gillian thought that the world wasn't exactly what she had thought. And neither were angels.

The next morning she stood and looked at herself in the mirror. She'd done this after Angel had first come to her and made her cut her hair—she'd wanted to look at her new self. Now she wanted to look at Gillian the Witch.

There wasn't anything overtly different about her. But now that she *knew*, she seemed to see things she hadn't noticed before. Something in the eyes—some ancient glimmer of knowledge in their depths. Something elfin in the face, in the slant of the cheekbones. A remnant of faery.

"Stop gazing and come shopping," Angel said, and light coalesced beside her.

"Right," Gillian said soberly. Then she tried to wiggle her nose.

Downstairs, she borrowed the keys to her mother's station wagon and bundled up. It was an icy-fresh day and the whole world sparkled under a light dusting of new snow. The air filled Gillian's lungs like some strange potion.

(I feel very witchy.) She backed the car out. (Now where do we go? Houghton?)

(Hardly. This isn't the kind of shopping you do at a mall. Northward, ho! We're going to Woodbridge.)

Gillian tried to remember Woodbridge. It was a little town like Somerset—but smaller. She'd undoubtedly driven through it at some point in her life.

(We need to go shopping in Woodbridge to take care of Tanya?)

(Just drive, dragonfly.)

Woodbridge's main street ended in a town square bordered by dozens of decorated trees. The stores were trimmed with Christmas lights. It was a postcard scene.

(Okay. Park here.)

Gillian followed Angel's directions and found herself in the Woodbridge Five and Ten, an old-style variety store, complete with creaking wooden floorboards. She had the terrifying feeling that time had gone back about fifty years. The aisles were tight and the shelves were jammed with baskets full of goods. There was a musty smell.

Beyond asking questions, she stared dreamily at a jar of penny candy.

(Head on to the back. All the way. Open that door and go through to the back room.)

Gillian nervously opened the rickety door and peered into the room beyond. But it was just another store. It had an even stranger smell, partly delicious, partly medicinal, and it was rather dimly lit.

"Uh, hello?" she said, in response to Angel's urging. And then she noticed movement behind a counter.

A girl was sitting there. She was maybe nineteen and had dark brown hair and an interesting face. It was quite ordinary in shape and structure—a country girl sort of face—but the eyes were unusually vivid and intense.

"Um, do you mind if I look around?" Gillian said, again in response to Angel.

"Go right ahead," the girl said. "I'm Melusine."

She watched with a perfectly friendly and open curiosity as Gillian moseyed around the shelves, trying to look as if she knew what she was looking for. Everything she saw was strange and unfamiliar—rocks and herby-looking things and different colored candles.

(It's not here.) Angel's voice was resigned. (We're going to have to ask her.)

"Excuse me," Gillian said a moment later, approaching the girl diffidently from the other side. "But do you have any Dragon's Blood? The—*activated* kind?"

The girl's face changed. She looked at Gillian very sharply. Then she said, "I'm afraid I've never heard of anything like that. And I wonder what makes you ask."

Gooseflesh blossomed on Gillian's arms. She had the sudden, distinct feeling that she was in danger.

CHAPTER 11

Angel's voice was taut but calm. (Pick up a pen from the counter. The black one's fine. Now—let go. Just relax and let me move it.)

Gillian let go. It was a process she couldn't have described in words if she'd tried. But she watched, with a sort of fascinated horror, as her own hand began to draw on a small white invoice slip.

It drew across the lines, in some kind of pattern. Unfortunately the pen seemed to be out of ink, so all Gillian could see was a faint scribble.

(Show her the carbon copy.)

Gillian peeled off the first sheet of paper. Underneath, in carbon, was her design. It looked like a flower—a dahlia. It was crudely colored in, as if it were meant to be dark.

(What is it, Angel?)

(A sort of password. Unless you know it, she's not going to let you buy what you need.)

Melusine's face had changed. She was looking at Gillian with startled interest.

"Unity," she said. "I *wondered* about you when you came in. You've got the look—but I've never seen you before. Did you just move here?"

(Say "Unity." It's their greeting. And tell her that you're just passing through.)

(Angel—is *she* a witch? Are there other witches around here? And how come I have to lie—)

(She's getting suspicious!)

The girl *was* looking at Gillian rather oddly. Like someone trying to catch a conversation. It scared Gillian.

"Unity. No, I'm just visiting," she said hastily. "And," she added as Angel whispered, "I need the Dragon's Blood and, um, two wax figures. Female. And do you have any charged Selket powder?"

Melusine settled back a little. "You belong to Circle Midnight." She said it flatly.

(Whaaaat? What's Circle Midnight? And how come she doesn't like me anymore?)

(It's a sort of witch organization. Like a club. It's the one that does the kind of spells that you need to do right now.)

(Aha. Bad spells, you mean.)

(Powerful spells. In your case, necessary spells.)

Melusine was scooting her chair behind the counter. For a moment Gillian wondered why she didn't get up, and then, as Melusine reached the edge of the counter, she understood. The chair was a wheelchair and Melusine's right leg was missing from the knee down.

It didn't seem to hinder her, though. In a moment, she was scooting back with a couple of packets and a box in her lap. She put the box on the counter and took out two dolls made of dull rose-colored wax. One of the packets held chunks of what looked like dark red chalk, the other a peacock-green powder.

She didn't look up as Gillian paid for the items. Gillian felt snubbed.

"Unity," she said formally, as she put her wallet away and gathered up her purchases. She figured if you said it for hello, you could say it for goodbye.

Melusine's dark eyes flashed up at her intently and almost quizzically. Then she said slowly, "Merry part . . . and merry meet again." It almost sounded like an invitation.

(Well, I'm lost.)

(Just say "Merry part" and get out of here, kid.)

Outside, Gillian looked at the town square with new eyes. (The Witches of Woodbridge. So, are they, like, all over here? Do they own the Creamery and the hardware store, too?)

(You're closer than you think. But we don't have time to stand around. You've got some spells to cast.)

Gillian took one more look around the quiet tree-lined square, feeling herself standing in the bright air with her packages of spell ingredients. Then she shook her head. She turned to the car.

Sitting in the middle of her bed with the bedroom door locked, Gillian contemplated her materials. The plastic bags of rock and powder, the dolls, and the hair she'd gathered from the brush in Macon's bathroom last night.

Two or three strands of sun-blond curls. Three or four long black glossy hairs.

"And you don't need to tell me what *they're* for," she said, looking at the air beside her. "It's voodoo time, huh?"

"Smart girl." Angel shimmered into being. "The hair is to personalize the dolls, to link them magically to their human counterparts. You've got to wind a hair around each doll, and name it out loud. Call it Tanya or Kimberlee."

Gillian didn't move. "Angel, look. When I got that hair, I had no idea why I was doing it. But when I saw those little wax figures—well, then I realized. And the way that girl Melusine looked at me. . . ."

"She has no idea what you're up against. Forget her."

"I'm just trying to get things straight, all right?" Hands clasped tightly in her lap, she looked at him. "I've never wanted to hurt people—well, all right, yes, I have. I've had those—those images or whatever at night, like seeing a giant foot splat down on my geometry teacher. But I don't *really* want to hurt people."

Angel looked patient. "Who said you were going to hurt them?"

"Well, what's all this *for*?"

"It's for whatever you want it to be for. Gillian, dragonfly, all these materials are just aids for a witch's natural powers. They're a way of focusing the power, directing it to a particular purpose. But what actually happens to Tanya and Kim depends on *you*. You don't have to hurt them. You just have to stop them."

"I just have to stop them from doing what they're planning to do." Gillian's mind was already sparking into action. "And Tanya's planning to write letters. And Kim's planning to spread the word. . . ."

"So what if Tanya can't write letters? And if Kimberlee can't talk? It would be sort of . . . poetic justice." Angel's face was grave, but his eyes were glinting with mischief.

Gillian bit her lip. "I think it would kill Kim not to talk!"

"Oh, I bet she could live through it." They were both laughing now. "So if she had, say, a bad sore throat . . . and if Tanya's arm were paralyzed . . ."

Gillian sobered. "Not paralyzed."

"I meant temporarily. Not even temporarily? All right, what about something else that could keep her from typing or holding a pen? How about a bad rash?"

"A rash?"

"Sure. An infection. One she'd have to keep bandaged up so she couldn't use her fingers. That would stop her for a while, until we can think of something else."

"A rash . . . Yeah, that could work. That would be good." Gillian took a quick breath and looked down at her materials. "Okay, tell me how to do it!"

And Angel walked her through the strange process. She wound the dolls with hair and named them aloud. She rubbed them with crumbled Dragon's Blood, the dark red chalky stuff. Then she dabbed the hand of one and the throat of the other with the iridescent green Selket powder.

"Now . . . may I be given the power of the words of Hecate. It is not I who utter them, it is not I who repeat them; it is Hecate who utters them, it is she who repeats them."

(And who the heck's Hecate?) She sent the thought to Angel wordlessly, in case speaking aloud would ruin the spell.

(Be quiet. Now concentrate. Pick up the Tanya doll and think *Streptococcus pyogenes*. That's a bacteria that'll give her a rash. Picture it in your mind. See the rash on the real Tanya.)

There was a certain satisfaction in doing it. Gillian couldn't deny that, even to herself. She pictured Tanya's slim olive-skinned right hand, poised to sign a letter that would destroy David's future. Then she pictured itchy red bumps appearing, another hand scratching. Redness spreading across the skin. More itching. More scratching . . .

(Hey, this is fun!)

Then she took care of the Kim doll.

When she was finished, she put both dolls in a shoe box and put the shoe box under her bed. Then she stood up, flushed and triumphant.

"It's over? I did it?"

"You did it. You're a full-fledged witch now. Hecate's the Queen of the Witches, incidentally. Their ancient ruler. And she's special to you—you're descended in a direct line from her daughter Hellewise."

"I am?" Gillian stood a little straighter. She seemed to feel power tingling through her, a sparkling energy, a sense that she could reach out and mold the world. She felt as if she ought to have an aura. "Really?"

"Your great-grandmother Elspeth was one of the Harmans, the Hearth-Women, the line that came from Hellewise. Elspeth's older sister Edgith became a big witch leader."

How could Gillian have ever thought she was ordinary, less than ordinary? You couldn't argue with facts like these. She was from a line of important witches. She was part of an ancient tradition. She was *special.*

She felt very, very powerful.

That night, her father called. He wanted to know if she was okay, and to let her know he loved her. All Gillian wanted to know was whether he'd be home for Christmas.

"Of course I'll be home. I love you."

"Love you."

But she wasn't happy when she hung up. (Angel, we've got to figure things out. Is there a spell I should do on *him*?)

(I'll think about it.)

The next morning she sailed into school cheerfully and looked around for someone who would talk. She spotted the cropped red head of J. Z. the Model and waved hello.

"What's up, J. Z.?"

J. Z. turned hazy blue-green eyes on her and fell into step. "Did you hear about Tanya?"

Gillian's heart skipped a beat. "No," she said, with perfect truth.

"She's got some awful rash or infection or something. Like poison ivy. They say it's driving her crazy." As always, J. Z. spoke slowly and with an almost vacant air. But Gillian thought there was a gleam of satisfaction under the blank look.

She shot J. Z. a sharp glance. "Well, that's too bad."

"Sure is," J. Z. murmured, smiling absently.

"I sure hope nobody else catches it." She was hoping to hear something about Kim.

But J. Z. just said, "Well, at least we know David won't." Then she wandered off.

(Angel, that girl doesn't like Tanya.)

(A lot of people don't like Tanya.)

(It's weird. I used to think being popular meant everybody

likes you. Now I think it's more like everybody's afraid *not* to like you.)

(Right. Let them hate you as long as they fear you. But, you see, you've done a public service, putting Tanya out of commission.)

In biology class, Gillian found out that Kim was absent and had canceled gymnastics practice for the day. She had something like strep throat and couldn't even talk. Nobody seemed heartbroken over this, either.

(Being popular means everybody's glad when something bad happens to you.)

(It's a dog-eat-dog world, kid.) Angel chuckled.

Gillian smiled.

She had protected David. It gave her a wonderful feeling to be able to protect him, to take care of him. Not that she exactly approved of what he'd done. Buying an English paper and turning it in as your own—that was pretty bad. Not just wrong, but petty somehow.

(But I think he was sorry. I think that was maybe one of the things he was saying he wasn't proud of. And maybe there's some way he can make up for it. Like if he wrote another paper and turned it in, and explained to Ms. Renquist. Don't you think, Angel?)

(Hm? Oh, sure. Good idea.)

(Because sometimes being sorry isn't enough, you know? You've got to *do* something. Angel? Angel?)

(I'm here. Just thinking about your next class. And your powers and things. Did you know there's a spell to bring in money?)

(There *is*? Now, that's really interesting. I mean, I don't care about *money* money, but I'd really love a car. . . .)

That night Gillian lay in bed, head propped on pillows, legs curled under a throw, and thought about how lucky she was.

Angel seemed to be gone for the moment; she could neither see him nor hear his voice. But it was Angel she was thinking about.

He had brought her so much—and he'd brought her *himself*, which she sometimes thought was the greatest gift of all. What other girl could have *two* gorgeous guys without being unfaithful to either of them, or making either of them jealous? What other girl could have two great loves at once, without doing wrong?

Because that was how she'd come to think of Angel. As a great love. He wasn't a pillar of light to her anymore, or a terrifyingly beautiful apparition with a voice like silver fire. He was almost like an ordinary guy, only impossibly handsome, devastatingly witty, and incidentally supernatural. Since learning she was supernatural herself, Gillian felt he was somehow more accessible.

And he understood her. Nobody had ever known her, or could ever know her, the way he did. He knew all her deepest secrets and most carefully hidden fears—and he still loved her.

The love was obvious every time he spoke to her, every time he appeared and looked at her with those startling eyes.

I'm in love with him, too, Gillian thought. She felt quite calm about it. It was different from the way she loved David. In a way, it was more powerful, because nobody could ever be as close to her as Angel was—but there was no physical aspect to it. Angel was a part of her on a level nothing human could touch. Their relationship was separate from the human world. It was unique.

"Tie me kangaroo down, mate!" A light was appearing beside the bed.

"Where've you been, Australia?"

"Checking on Tanya and Kim the Gym, actually. Tanya's bandaged from shoulder to fingers and she's not thinking about writing *anything*. Kim's sucking a popsicle and moaning. Inaudibly."

"Good." Gillian felt a triumphant glow. Which was wrong, of course; she shouldn't *enjoy* other people's pain. But she couldn't hide it from Angel—and those girls deserved it. They would be sorry, sorry, sorry they had ever tangled with Gillian Lennox.

"But we've got to work out a more permanent solution," she said. "And figure things out about my parents."

"I'm working on all of it." Angel was gazing at her with a kind of dreamy intentness.

"What?"

"Nothing. Just looking at you. You look particularly beautiful tonight, which is absurd considering you're wearing flannel pajamas with bears on them."

Gillian felt a quick sweet throb. She looked down. "These are cats. But the bears are my favorite, actually." She looked back up and grinned wickedly. "I'll bet I could start a little bears fashion at school. You can do anything with enough guts."

"*You* can do anything, that's for sure. Sweet dreams, beautiful."

"Silly. Stop it." Gillian waved a hand at him. But she was still blushing when she lay down and shut her eyes. She felt absurdly happy and complimented. And beautiful. And powerful. And special.

"Hear about Tanya?" Amanda the Cheerleader said at lunch break the next day. She and Gillian were in the girls' bathroom.

Gillian eyed herself in the mirror. A touch with the comb . . . perfect. And maybe a little more lipstick. She was doing the glamour thing today. Dark, mesmerizing eyes and bold, laughing red mouth. Or maybe she should pout instead of laugh. She pursed her lips at herself and said absently, "Old news."

"No, I mean the new stuff. She's got complications, apparently."

Gillian stopped applying lipstick. "What kind of complications?"

"I don't know. Fever, I think. And her whole arm's turning purple."

(Angel? *Purple?*)

(Well, I'd say more mauve myself. Relax, kid. Fever's a natural side effect of a bad rash. Just like poison ivy.)

(But—)

(Look at Amanda. *She's* not too upset.)

(No, 'cause she probably knows Tanya was messing with her boyfriend. Or she has some other reason not to like her. But, I mean, I don't want Tanya *really* hurt.)

(Don't you? Be honest.)

(Well, I mean, not really, *really* hurt, you know? Medium hurt. That's all.)

(I don't think she's going to drop dead this minute.) Angel said it patiently.

(Okay. Good.) Gillian felt a little embarrassed for making a big deal—and at the same time she had a fleeting impulse to go check on Tanya herself. But the impulse was easily quashed. Tanya was getting what she deserved. It was only a rash. How bad could that be?

Besides, Angel was looking after things. And she trusted Angel.

She added the last dab of lipstick and smiled at herself in the mirror. Definitely she was one hot witch.

In sixth period, messengers brought candy canes that people had ordered last week from the Vocal Jazz Club. You could send the candy canes, which came with a ribbon and a note, to anyone you wanted.

Gillian got a pile so large that everyone laughed, and Seth Pyles ran over and snapped a picture of it for the yearbook. After school David came and rummaged through the pile, looking at the messages and shaking his fist, pretending to be jealous.

It was a very good day.

"Happy?" Angel asked that afternoon. David's mother had recruited him for heavy-duty Christmas housecleaning, so Gillian was alone in her bedroom—which meant it was just her and Angel. She was folding socks and humming her favorite carol, "O Come All Ye Faithful."

"Can't you tell?"

"Not with all that noise you're making. Are you really happy?"

She looked up. "Of course I am. I mean, except for the stuff with my parents, I'm totally happy."

"And being popular is all you expected it to be."

"Well . . ." Gillian paused in bewilderment. "It's—it's a little *different* from what I expected. It's not the be-all and the end-all I'd have thought. But then *I'm* different from what I thought."

"You're a witch. And you want more than just candy canes and parties."

She looked at him curiously. "What are you trying to say? That I should do some more spells?"

"I'm saying that there's more to being a witch than doing spells. I can show you, if you trust me."

CHAPTER 12

"Yes," Gillian said simply. Her heart rate had picked up a little, but with anticipation rather than fear. Angel was looking very mysterious.

He struck a looking-into-the-distance pose, then said, "Have you ever had the feeling that you don't really know reality?"

"Frequently," Gillian said dryly. "Ever since I met you."

He grinned. "I mean even before that. Someone wrote about the 'inconsolable secret' that's in each of us. The desire for our own far-off country, for something we've never actually experienced. About how we all long 'to bridge some chasm that yawns between us and reality . . . to be reunited with something in the universe from which we now feel cut off. . . .'"

Gillian sat bolt upright. "*Yes.* I never heard anybody say it that well before. About the chasm—you always feel that there's something else, *somewhere*, and that you're being left out. I thought it was something the popular people would be in on—but it hasn't got anything to do with them at all."

"As if the world has some secret, if you could only get on the inside."

"Yes. Yes." She looked at him in fascination. "This is about being a witch, isn't it? You're saying that I've always felt that way because it's *true*. Because for me there is a different reality. . . ."

"Nah." Angel grimaced. "Actually everybody feels exactly the same. Doesn't mean a thing."

Gillian collapsed. *"What?"*

"For them. For them, there is no secret place. As for you . . . well, it's not what you're thinking; it's not some higher reality of astral planes or anything. It's as real as those socks. As real as that girl, Melusine, in the store in Woodbridge. And it's where you were meant to be. A place where you'll be welcomed into the heart of things."

Gillian's heart was racing wildly. "Where is it?"

"It's called the Night World."

Gray-blue shadows were gliding up the hills. Gillian drove in the twilight, heading toward the darkness in the east.

"Explain again," she said, and she said it out loud, even though she couldn't see Angel. There was a slight disturbance of air above the seat to her right, a hint of mist, but that was all. "You're saying it's not just witches."

"Not by a long shot. Witches are just one race; there are all sorts of other creatures of the night. All the sorts that you've been taught to think are legends."

"And they're *real*. And they're just living alongside normal humans. And they always have been."

"Yes. But it's easy, you see. They look like humans, at least at first glance. As much as *you* look like a human."

"But I *am* a human. I mean, mostly, right? My great-grandma was a witch, but she married a human and so did my grandma and my mom. So I'm all . . . diluted."

"It doesn't matter to them. You can claim witch blood. And your powers are beyond dispute. Trust me, they'll welcome you."

"Besides, I've got *you*," Gillian said cheerfully. "I mean, ordinary humans don't have their own invisible guardians, do they?"

"Well." Angel seemed to coalesce dimly beside her. From what she could see of his face, he was frowning. "You can't actually tell them about me. Don't ask why; I'm not allowed to explain. But I'll be with you, the way I always am. I'll help you out with what to say. Don't worry; you'll do fine."

Gillian wasn't worried. She felt steeped in mystery and a sort of forbidden excitement. The whole world seemed magical and unfamiliar.

Even the snow looked different, blue and almost phosphorescent. As Gillian drove through rolling farmlands, a glow appeared above the eastern hills, and then the full moon rose, huge and throbbing with light.

Deeper and deeper, she thought. She seemed to have left everything ordinary behind and to be sliding more and more quickly into an enchanted place where anything—anything at all—could happen.

She wouldn't have been surprised if Angel had directed her to pull off into some snowy clearing and look for a fairy ring. But when he said, "Turn here," it was at a main road that led to the straggling outskirts of a town.

"Where are we?"

"Sterback. Little hole-in-the-wall place—except for where we're going. Stop here."

"Here" was a nondescript building, which looked as if it had originally been Victorian. It wasn't in very good repair.

Gillian got out and looked at the moon shining on the windows. The building might have been a lodge. It was set apart from the rest of the dark and silent town. A wind had started up and she shivered.

(Uh, it doesn't look like anybody's in there.)

(Go to the door.) Angel's voice in her mind was comforting, as always.

There was no sign at the door, nothing to indicate that this was a public building. But the stained glass window above the door was faintly illuminated from the inside. The pattern seemed to be a flower. A black iris.

(The Black Iris is the name of this place. It's a club—)

Angel was interrupted by a sudden explosion. That was Gillian's impression. For the first instant she had no idea what it was—just a dark shape flying at her and a violent noise—and she almost fell off the porch. Then she realized that the noise was barking. A chained dog was yammering and foaming, trying to get at her.

(I'll take care of it.) Angel sounded grim, and an instant later Gillian felt something like a wave in the air. The dog dropped flat as if it had been shot. It rolled its eyes.

The porch was dead silent again. Everything was silent. Gillian stood and breathed, feeling adrenaline run through her. But before she could say anything, the door opened behind her.

A face looked out of the dimness inside the house. Gillian couldn't make out the features, but she could see the gleam of eyes.

"Who're you?" The voice was slow and flat, not friendly. "What do you want?"

Gillian followed Angel's whispered words. "I'm Gillian of the Harman clan, and I want *in*. It's *cold* out here."

"A Harman?"

"I'm a Hearth-Woman, a daughter of Hellewise, and if you don't let me in, you stupid werewolf, I'm going to do to you what I did to your cousin there." She stuck out a gloved finger toward the cringing dog. (Werewolf? Angel, there are real werewolves?)

(I told you. All the legendary creatures.)

Gillian felt an odd sinking. She had no idea why, and she continued to do just as Angel said. But somehow her stomach was knotting tighter and tighter.

The door opened slowly. Gillian stepped into a dim hall and the door slammed shut again with a curiously final sound.

"Didn't recognize you," the figure beside her said. "Thought you might be vermin."

"I forgive you," Gillian said, and pulled off her gloves at Angel's direction. "Downstairs?"

He nodded and she followed him to a door that led to a stairway. As soon as the door opened, Gillian heard music.

She descended, feeling extremely . . . subterranean. The basement was deeper than most basements. And bigger. It was like a whole new world down there.

It wasn't much brighter than upstairs, and there were no windows. It seemed like an *old* place; there was a shuffleboard pattern on the cold tile floor and a faint smell of mildew and moisture. But it was alive with people. There were figures sitting on chairs clumped around the borders of the room and more gathered around a pool table at one end. There were figures in front of a couple of ancient-looking pinball machines and figures clustered at what looked like a home bar.

Gillian headed for the bar. She could feel eyes on her every step of the way.

She felt too small and too young as she perched precariously on one of the bar stools. She rested her elbows on the counter and tried to slow her heart down.

The figure behind the bar turned toward her. It was a guy, maybe in his twenties. He stepped forward and Gillian saw his face.

Shock rippled through her. There was something . . . *wrong* with him. Not that he was hideously ugly or that he would have caused a commotion if he got on a bus. Maybe it was something Gillian sensed through her new powers and not through her eyes at all. But the impression she got was that his face looked *wrong*. Tainted by cold, dark thoughts that made Tanya's scheming mind look like a sunlit garden.

Gillian couldn't help her recoil. And the bar guy saw it.

"You're new," he said. The dark and cold seemed to grow in him and she realized he was enjoying her fear. "Where are you from?"

Angel was shouting instructions at her. "I'm a Harman," Gillian said as steadily as she could. "And—you're right. I'm new."

(Good, kid. Don't let him bully you! Now you're going to explain to them just exactly who you are—)

(In a minute, Angel. Just let me get—settled.) The truth was that Gillian was completely unsettled. The sense of dread that had been growing ever since she walked in was reaching an unbearable pitch. This place was . . . she groped for adjectives. Unwholesome. Corrupt. Scary.

And then she realized something else. Up until now she hadn't been able to make out the faces of the other figures properly. Only eyes and the occasional flash of teeth.

But now—they were moving in around her. It reminded her of sharks, swimming almost aimlessly but ending up in a purposeful gathering. There were people directly behind her— she could feel that with the back of her neck—and there were people on either side of her. When she looked, she could see their faces.

Cold—dark—wrong. Not just wrong, but almost diabolic. These were people who might do anything and enjoy it. Their eyes glittered at her. More than glittered. Some of the eyes were *shining* . . . like an animal's at night . . . and now they were smiling and she could see *teeth*. Long delicate canine teeth that came to a point. *Fangs* . . .

All the legendary creatures . . .

Sheer panic surged through her. And at the same instant, she felt strong hands on her elbows.

"Why don't you come outside with me?" a voice behind her said.

Then things were confused. Angel was yelling again, but Gillian couldn't really hear him over the pounding of her own heart. The hands were exerting pressure, forcing her away from the bar. And the figures with their diabolical faces were settling back, most of them wearing conspiratorial grins.

"Have fun," somebody called.

Gillian was being hurried up the stairs, whisked through the dim building. A blast of cold air hit her as the door opened and she suddenly felt clearer. She tried to break out of the iron grip that was holding her. It didn't do any good.

She was out in the snow, leaving the house behind. The street was completely deserted.

"Is that your car?"

The hands on her arms eased their pressure. Gillian gave one desperate wrench and turned around.

Moonlight was shining on the snow around her, giving it the texture of white satin. Every shadow was like an indigo stain on the sparkling coverlet.

The person who'd been holding her was a boy a few years older than Gillian. He was lanky and elegant, with ash-blond hair and slightly tilted eyes. Something about the way he held himself made her think of lazy predatory animals.

But his face wasn't *wrong*, the way the other faces had been. It was set and grim, maybe even a little scary, but it wasn't evil.

"Now, look," he said, and his voice wasn't evil, either, just rapid and short. "I don't know who you are, or how you managed to get in there, but you'd better turn around and go home right now. Because whatever you are, you're not a Harman."

"How do you know?" Gillian blurted before Angel could tell her what to say.

"Because I'm related to the Harmans. I'm Ash Redfern.

You don't even know what that means, do you? If you *were* a Harman you'd know that our families are kin."

(You *are* a Harman, and you *are* a witch!) Angel was actually raging. (Tell him! Tell him!)

But the ash-blond boy was going on. "They'll eat you alive in there if they find out for sure. They're not as—tolerant—of humans as I am. So my advice is, get in your car, drive away, and never come back. And never mention this place to anybody else."

(You're a lost witch! You're not a human. Tell him!)

"How come *you're* so tolerant?" Gillian was staring at the boy. His eyes . . . she'd thought they were amber-colored originally, like Steffi's, but now they were emerald green.

He gave her an odd look. Then he smiled. It was a lazy smile, but with something heart-wrenching behind it.

"I met a human girl last summer," he said quietly, and that seemed to explain everything.

Then he nodded at her car. "Get out of here. Never come back. I'm just passing through; I won't be around to save you again."

(Don't get in the car. Don't go. Tell him. You're a witch; you belong to Circle Midnight. *Don't go!*)

For the first time, Gillian deliberately disobeyed an order of Angel's. She unlocked the car with shaky hands. As she got in, she looked back at the boy. Ash.

"Thank you," she said.

"Bye." He wiggled his fingers. He watched as she drove away.

(Go back there right now! You *belong* there, just as much as any of them. You're one of them. They can't keep you out. Turn around and go back!)

"Angel, stop it!" She said it out loud. "I can't! Don't you see that? I *can't*. They were *horrible*. They were—*evil*."

Now that she was alone, reaction was setting in. Her whole body began to shake. She was suddenly blind with tears, her breath catching in her throat.

"Not evil!" Angel shimmered into the seat beside her. He had never sounded so agitated. "Just powerful—"

"They were *evil*. They wanted to hurt me. I saw their eyes!" She was lapsing into hysteria. "Why did you *take* me there? You wouldn't even let me talk to Melusine. Melusine wasn't like *them*."

A violent shiver overtook her. The car veered and she struggled with it, barely getting control. All at once everything seemed alien and terrifying; she was out on a long and lonely road, and it was night, and there was an uncanny *being* in the seat beside her.

She didn't know who he was anymore. All she knew was that he wasn't any kind of an angel. The logical alternative sprang immediately to her mind. She was alone in the middle of nowhere *with a demon. . . .*

"Gillian, stop it!"

"Who are you? What are you, really? *Who are you?*"

"What do you mean? You know who I am."

"No, I don't!" She was screaming it. "I don't know any-thing about you! Why did you take me there? Why did you want them to hurt me? Why?"

"Gillian, stop the car. *Stop. The. Car.*"

His voice was so commanding, so urgent and imperative, that she actually obeyed. She was sobbing anyway. She couldn't drive or see. She felt, literally and honestly, that she was losing her mind at that exact moment.

"Now look at me. Wipe your face off and look at me."

After a moment she managed. He was shining. Light seemed to radiate from every inch of him, from the gold fila-ments of his hair, to his classic features, to the lines of his per-fect body. And he'd calmed down. His expression was rapt and uplifted, the serenity only marred by what looked like concern for her.

"Now," he said. "I'm sorry if all this scared you. New things are like that sometimes—they seem repulsive just because they're different. But we won't talk about that now," he added, as Gillian caught a shuddering breath. "The important thing is that I wasn't trying to hurt you." His eyes seemed to grow even more intense, pure violet flame.

Gillian hiccupped. "But—you—"

"I could *never* hurt you, Gillian. Because, you see, we're soulmates."

He said it with the weight of a monumental revelation. And although Gillian had no idea what it meant, she felt an odd quiver inside, almost of recognition.

"What's that?"

"It's something that happens with people who belong to the Night World. It means that there's only one love for everyone who exists. And when you meet that love, you know them. You know you were meant to be together, and nothing can keep you apart."

It was true. Every word seemed to resonate inside Gillian, touching off ancient, hidden memories. This was something her ancestors had known.

Her cheeks had dried. Her hysteria was gone. But she felt very tired and very bewildered.

"But . . . if that's true . . ." She couldn't put the thought together.

"Don't worry about it right now." Angel's voice was soothing. "We'll talk about it later. I'll explain what it all means. I just wanted you to know that I would never hurt you. I love you, Gillian. Don't you realize that?"

"Yes," Gillian whispered. Everything was very foggy. She didn't want to think, didn't want to consider the implications of what Angel was saying.

She just wanted to get home.

"Relax and I'll help you drive," Angel said. "Don't worry about anything. It's all going to be all right."

CHAPTER 13

The next day, Gillian tried to concentrate on normal things.

She hurried to school, feeling unrested—had she had nightmares?—and desperately in need of distraction. All day at school, she threw herself into activities, chattering and laughing and keeping people around her, talking about Christmas and parties and finals.

It worked. Angel was very gentle, keeping quietly in the background. All the other students were hyperactive with the thought of only two more days of school. And by the afternoon Gillian had become caught up in her own frantic good spirits.

"We don't even have a tree," she said to David. "And it's five days to Christmas Eve. I have to drag my mom out and buy one."

"Don't buy one," David said, smiling at her with his dark

eyes. "I'll take you out tonight to a place I know. It's beautiful, and the trees are free." He winked.

"I'll bring the station wagon," Gillian said. "Lots of room. I like *big* trees."

At home, she stayed busy, prodding her mother to wrap packages and dust off the plastic Christmas flower arrangements. There was no talk with Angel about how to tell her mother about witches.

She was still happy when she picked David up after dinner. He seemed a little subdued, but she wasn't in the mood to ask questions. Instead, she talked about the party Steffi Lockhart was giving on Friday night.

It was a long drive, and she was running out of speculations about Steffi's party when David finally said, "Somewhere along here, I think."

"Okay. I'll take one of those." Gillian pointed at the sixty-foot-tall pine trees that lined the road.

David smiled. "There are some smaller ones farther in."

There were so many that Gillian had a hard time choosing. At last, she settled on a balsam fir with a perfect silhouette, like a plump lady holding out her skirts. It was wonderfully aromatic as she and David chopped it down and half dragged, half carried it to the car.

"I just love that smell," she said. "And I don't even care that my gloves are ruined."

David didn't answer. He was quiet as he tied the back of

the station wagon closed around the tree. He was quiet as they got in the car and Gillian began to drive.

And Gillian couldn't stand it anymore. Little waves of acid were lapping in her stomach. "What's wrong? You haven't been talking all night."

"I'm sorry." He let out his breath, looking out the window. "I guess . . . I was just thinking about Tanya."

Gillian blinked. "Tanya? Should I be jealous?"

He glanced at her. "No, I mean—her arm."

A strange sort of prickling cascaded over Gillian, and in that moment everything changed forever. She seemed to ask the next question in a huge, quivering stillness. "What about her arm?"

"You didn't hear? I thought somebody would've called you. They took her to the hospital this afternoon."

"Oh, my God."

"Yeah, but it's worse. That thing they thought was a rash was necrotizing something-or-other . . . you know, that flesh-eating bacteria."

Gillian opened her mouth, but no sound came out. The road in front of her seemed very dim.

"Cory said she can't have any visitors—her arm swelled up to three times its normal size. They had to cut it open all the way from her shoulder to her finger to drain it. They think she might lose her finger—"

"Stop it!" A suppressed scream.

David looked at her quickly. "I'm sorry—"

"No! Just don't talk!" Gillian's automatic reflexes had taken over driving the car. She was hardly aware of anything outside her own body. All her concentration was fixed on the drama inside her own mind.

(Angel! Did you hear that? What is going *on*?)

(Of course I heard it.) The voice was slow and thoughtful.

(Well, is it true? Is it?)

(Look, let's talk about this later, all right, kid? Let's wait—)

(No! Everything with you is "Wait" or "We'll talk about it later." I want to know *right now*: is it true?)

(Is what true?)

(*Is Tanya that sick?* Is she about to lose her *finger*?)

(It's just an infection, Gillian. *Streptococcus pyogenes*. You were the one who put it there.)

(You're saying it *is* true. It's true. I did it with *my* spell. I gave her flesh-eating bacteria.) Gillian threw the thoughts out wildly, disjointedly. She couldn't really grasp what it all meant yet.

(Gillian, we had to stop her from destroying David. It was necessary.)

(No! No! You knew I didn't really want to hurt her. What are you *talking* about? How can you even *say* that?) Gillian was in hysteria again, a strange hysteria of the mind. She was vaguely aware that she was still driving, that fences and trees were flying by. Her body was sitting in the car, breathing quickly, speeding, but her real self seemed to be in another place.

(You lied to me. You told me she was all right. Why did you do that?)

(Calm down, dragonfly—)

(*Don't call me that!* How can you just—just sit there . . . and not care? What kind of person *are* you?)

And then—Angel's voice changed. He didn't get hysterical or agitated; it was much worse. His voice became calmer. More melodious. Pleasant.

(I'm just dispensing justice. It's what angels do, you know.)

Icy horror swept over Gillian.

He sounded insane.

"Oh, God," she said, and she said it out loud. David looked at her.

"Hey—are you okay?"

She scarcely heard him. She was thinking with fevered intensity: (I don't know *what* you are, but you are *not* an angel.)

(Gillian, listen to me. We don't have to fight. I *love* you—)

(Then tell me how to fix Tanya!)

Silence.

(I'll find out myself. I'll go back to Melusine—)

(No!)

(Then tell me! Or heal Tanya yourself if you're a real angel!)

A pause. Then: (Gillian, I've got an idea. A way to make David love you more.)

(What are you *talking* about?)

(We need to give him a near-death experience. Then he'll be able to truly understand you. We need to make him die.)

Everything blurred. Gillian knew they were nearing Somerset, they were on familiar streets. But for a moment her vision went completely gray and sparkling.

"Gillian!" A hand was on hers, a real hand, steadying the wheel. "Are you all right? Do you want me to drive?"

"I'm okay." Her vision had cleared. She just wanted to get home. She had to get to that shoe box and fix the spell on Tanya somehow. She had to get home . . . to safety. . . .

But nowhere was safe.

(Don't you understand?) The voice was soft and insidious in her ear. (David can never really be like you until he's died the way you have. We have to make him die—)

"No!" She realized she was speaking aloud again. "Stop talking to me! Go away!"

David was staring at her. "Gillian—"

(I don't want to hurt you, Gillian. Only him. And he'll come back, I promise. He might be a little different. But he'll still love you.)

Different . . . *David's body.* Angel wanted David's body. As David left, Angel would take possession. . . .

They were almost home. But she couldn't get away from the voice. How do you get away from something that's *in your own mind*? She couldn't shut it out. . . .

(Just let go, Gillian. Let me take over. I'll drive for you. I love you, Gillian.)

"No!" She was panting, her hands gripping the steering wheel so hard it hurt. The word came out jerkily. "David! You have to drive. I can't—"

(Relax, Gillian. You won't be harmed. I promise.)

And she couldn't let go of the steering wheel. The voice seemed to be inside her body, diffusing through her muscles. She couldn't take her foot off the accelerator.

"Gillian, slow down!" David was yelling now. "Look out!"

(It will only take a second . . .)

Gillian's world had been switched into an old-time movie. The flickering black-and-white kind. With each frame, the telephone pole in front of her got bigger and bigger. It was happening very slowly, but at the same time with utter inevitability. They were rushing oh-so-slowly toward that pole, and they were going to hit. On the right side of the car, where David was sitting.

(No! I'll hate you *forever* . . .)

She screamed it in her mind and the last word seemed to echo endlessly. There was time for that.

And then there was a loud sound and darkness.

"Can I see him?"

"Not yet, honey." Her mother scooted the plastic chair closer to the emergency room bed. "Probably not tonight."

"But I *have* to."

"Gillian, he's unconscious. He wouldn't even know you were there."

"But I have to *see* him." Gillian felt the hysteria swelling again, and she clamped her mouth shut. She didn't want a shot, which is what the nurses had said they were going to give her when she started screaming earlier.

She had been here for hours. Ever since the cars with the flashing lights came and pried the station wagon door open and pulled her out. They'd pulled David out, too. But while she had been completely unhurt—"A miracle! Not even a scratch!" the paramedic had said to her mother—David had been unconscious. And had stayed that way ever since.

The emergency room was cold and it didn't seem to matter how many heated blankets they wrapped around her. Gillian kept shivering. Her hands were blue-white and pinched-looking.

"Daddy's coming home," her mother said, stroking her arm. "He's taking the first plane he could get. You'll see him tomorrow morning."

Gillian shivered. "Is this the same hospital—where Tanya Jun is? No, don't answer. I don't really want to know." She stuck her hands under her armpits. "I'm so cold. . . ."

And alone. There was no soft voice in her head. And that was *good*, because, God, the last thing she wanted was Angel— or rather that *thing*, whatever it was, that monster that had called itself an angel. But it was strange after so long. To be all alone . . . and not know where *he* might be lurking. He could be listening to her thoughts right now. . . .

"I'll get another blanket." The nurse had shown her mother the heated closet. "If you could just lie down, honey, maybe you'd feel like sleeping a little."

"I can't sleep! I have to go see David."

"Hon, I already told you. You're not going to see him tonight."

"You said I *might* not get to see him. You didn't say I *wouldn't*! You only said *probably*!" Gillian's voice was rising, getting more shrill, and there was nothing she could do about it. The tears were coming, too, flooding down uncontrollably. She was choking on them.

A nurse came hurrying in, the white curtains around the bed swirling. "It's all right; it's natural," she said softly to Gillian's mother. And to Gillian: "Now, just lean over a little—hold still. A little pinch. This is something to help you relax."

Gillian felt a sting at her hip. A short time later everything got blurry and the tears stopped.

She woke up in her own bed.

It was morning. Pale sunlight was shining full in the window.

Last night . . . oh, yes. She could vaguely remember her

mom and Mrs. Beeler, their next-door neighbor, leading her from the hospital to Mrs. Beeler's car. She remembered them taking her upstairs and undressing her and putting her to bed. After that she'd had hours of wonderful not-thinking.

And now she was awake and rested and her head was clear. She knew exactly what she had to do even before she swung her legs out from under the covers.

She glanced at the ancient Snoopy clock on her nightstand and got a shock. Twelve thirty-five. No wonder she was rested.

Efficiently, without making a sound, she put on Levis and a gray sweatshirt. No makeup. She ran a comb once through her hair.

She paused, then, to listen. Not just to the house, but to herself. To the world inside her own brain.

Dead quiet. Not a creature stirring. Not that that meant a thing, of course.

Gillian knelt and pulled the shoe box out from under her bed. The wax dolls were garish, red and green, like a hideous parody of Christmas. Her first impulse at the sight of that poisonous green was to get rid of it. Snap off one doll's hand and the other's head.

But what that would do to Tanya and Kim, she didn't want to think. Instead, she forced herself to get a Q-tip from the bathroom, soak it in water, and dab the iridescent green powder away.

She cried as she did it. She tried to concentrate as she had when she'd done the spell, seeing the real Tanya's hand, seeing it heal and become whole.

"Now may I be given the power of the words of Hecate," she whispered. "It is not I who utter them, it is not I who repeat them; it is Hecate who utters them, it is she who repeats them."

When the powder was off, she put the dolls back in the box. Then she blew her nose and rummaged through the pile on her desk until she found a small pink-flowered address book.

She sat on the floor cross-legged, dragged the phone close, and thumbed through the book.

There.

Daryl Novak's cellular phone number.

She dialed quickly and shut her eyes. Answer. Answer.

"Hello," a languid voice said.

Her eyes flew open. "Daryl, this is Gillian. I need you to do me an enormous favor, and I need you to do it *now*. And I can't even explain why—"

"Gillian, are you okay? Everybody's been worried about you."

"I'm fine, but I can't talk. I need you to go find Amy Nowick; she's got"—Gillian thought frantically—"uh, honors chemistry this period. I need you to tell her to drive to the corner of Hazel and Applebutter Street and wait for me there."

"You want her to leave school?"

"Right now. Tell her I know it's a lot to ask, but I *need* this. It's really important."

She expected questions. But instead, all Daryl said was, "Leave it to me. I'll find her."

"Thanks, Daryl. You're a lifesaver."

Gillian hung up and found her ski jacket. Tucking the shoe box under her arm, she walked very quietly downstairs.

She could hear voices from the kitchen. A low voice—her dad's. Part of her wanted to run to him.

But what would her parents do if they saw her? Keep her safe and bundled up, keep her *here*. They wouldn't understand what she had to do.

There was no question of telling them the truth, of course. That would just get her another shot. And, eventually, maybe a visit to the mental hospital where her mother had stayed. Everyone would think delusions ran in the family.

She moved stealthily to the front door, quietly opened it, slipped out.

Sometime during the night it had rained and then frozen. Ice hung like dewdrops from the twigs of the hickory tree in the yard.

Gillian ducked her head and hurried down the street. She hoped no one was watching, but she had the feeling of eyes staring from between bare branches and out of shadows.

At the corner of Hazel and Applebutter she stood with her arms wrapped around the box, hopping a little to keep warm.

It's a lot to ask . . .

It *was* a lot to ask, especially considering the way she'd treated Amy recently. And it was funny, considering all the new friends she'd made, that it was Amy she turned to instinctively when she was in trouble.

But . . . there was something solid and genuine and *good* in Amy. And Gillian knew that she would show up.

The Geo swung around the corner and skidded to a stop. Typical Amy-without-glasses driving. Then Amy was jumping out, her face turned anxiously toward Gillian's. Her blue eyes were huge and seemed luminous with tears.

And then they were hugging and crying. Both of them.

"I'm so sorry. I've been so rotten this last week—"

"But I was rotten to you before that—"

"I feel *awful.* You have every right to be mad at me—"

"Ever since I heard about the accident, I've been so *worried.*"

Gillian pulled back. "I can't stay. I don't have time. And I know how this sounds coming from somebody who hit a pole last night . . . but I need your car. For one thing, I've got to go see David."

Amy nodded, blotting her eyes. "Say no more."

"I can drop you off at home—"

"It's the wrong way. It won't hurt me to walk. I *want* to walk."

Gillian almost laughed. The sight of Amy dabbing her face with her muffler and stamping her foot on the icy sidewalk, determined to walk, warmed her heart.

She hugged her again, fast. "Thank you. I'll never forget

it. And I'll never be the terrible person I've been to you again, at least—"

She broke off and got in the car. She'd been about to finish the sentence "—at least, if I live through this."

Because she wasn't at all sure that she would.

But the first thing was to get to David.

She had to see him with her own eyes. To make sure he was all right . . . and that he was himself.

She gunned the motor and set out for Houghton.

CHAPTER 14

She got David's room number from a receptionist at the front desk. She didn't ask if she was allowed to visit.

All Gillian could think as she walked down the hall was, *Please.* Please, if David was only all right, there was a chance that everything could work out.

At the door she stopped and held her breath.

Her mind was showing her all sorts of pictures. David in a coma, hooked up to so many tubes and wires that he was unrecognizable. Worse, David alive and awake and smiling . . . and looking at her with violet eyes.

She knew what Angel's plan had been. At least, she thought she knew. The only question was, had he succeeded?

Still holding her breath, she looked around the door.

David was sitting up in bed. The only thing he was hooked up to was an IV of clear fluid. There was another bed in the room, empty.

He looked toward the door and saw her.

Gillian walked toward him slowly. She kept her face absolutely expressionless, her eyes on him.

Dark hair. A lean face that still had traces of a summer tan. Cheekbones to die for and eyes to drown in. . . .

But no half-quizzical, half-friendly smile. He was looking back at her as soberly as she was looking at him, a book slipping unnoticed from his lap.

Gillian reached the foot of the hospital bed. They stared at each other.

What do I *say*? David, is it really you? I can't. It's too stupid, and what's he going to say back? No, dragonfly, it's not him, it's me?

The silence stretched on. At last, very quietly, the guy on the bed said, "Are you okay?"

"Yeah." The word came out clipped and dispassionate. "Are *you* okay?"

"Yeah, pretty much. I was lucky." He was watching her. "You look—kind of different."

"And you're kind of quiet."

Something like puzzlement flashed in his eyes. Then something like hurt. "I was . . . well, you walked in here looking so deadpan, and you sound so . . . cold . . ." He shook his head slightly, his eyes fixed on hers. "Gillian—did I do something to make you want to hit that pole?"

"I didn't do it on purpose!" She found herself lunging forward, reaching for his hands.

He looked startled. "Okay . . ."

"David, I *didn't*. I was doing everything I could *not* to. I would never want to hurt you. Don't you know that?"

His face cleared. His eyes were very dark but very calm. "Yes, I do," he said simply. "I believe you."

Strangely, she knew he did. In spite of all the evidence to the contrary, he believed her.

Gillian's hands tightened on his. Their eyes were locked together. It was as if they were getting closer, although neither of them moved physically.

And then it was all happening, what had started to happen at least twice before. Feelings so sweet and strong she could hardly bear it. Strange recognition, unexpected belonging . . . impossible knowing . . .

Gillian's eyes seemed to shut of their own accord. And then somehow they were kissing. She felt the warmth of David's lips. And everything was warm and wonderful . . . but there was more.

It was as if the normal veil that separated two people had melted.

Gillian felt a shock of revelation. *This* was what it meant, what Angel had spoken to her about. She knew it intuitively even though she'd never spoken the word before.

Soulmates.

She'd found hers. The one love for her on this earth. The person she was *meant* to be with, that no one could keep her from. And it wasn't Angel. It was David.

That was the other thing she knew, and knew with a bedrock certainty that nothing could touch. *This* was David, the true David. He was holding her in his arms, kissing her. Her, the ordinary Gillian, who was wearing an old gray sweatshirt and no makeup.

It was absurd that she'd ever believed things like makeup mattered.

David was alive, *that* was what mattered. Gillian didn't have his death on her conscience. And if they could somehow live through the rest of what had to be done, they just might be happier than she had ever imagined.

How weird that she could still think. But they didn't seem to be kissing anymore; they were just holding each other now. And that was almost as good, just feeling his body against hers.

Gillian pulled away.

"David—"

His eyes were full of wonder. "You know what? I love you."

"I know." Gillian realized she was being less than romantic. She couldn't help it. This was the time for action. "David, I have to tell you some things, and I don't know if you can believe me. But you've got to try."

"Gillian, I said I love you. I *mean* that. We—" Then he stopped and searched her face. He seemed to see something that changed his mind. "I love you," he said in a different tone. "So I'll believe you."

"The first thing is that I'm not anything like what you

think. I'm not brave, or noble, or witty in the face of danger or—or *anything* like that. It's all been—a sort of setup. And here's how it happened."

And then she told him.

Everything. From the beginning, from the afternoon when she'd heard the crying in the woods and followed it and died and found an angel.

She told him the whole story, about how Angel had appeared in her room that night and how he'd changed her whole life. About the whispering that had guided her ever since.

And about the *very* bad things. Her witch heritage. The spell she'd put on Tanya. The Night World. All the way up to the accident last night.

When she was done, she sat back and looked at him.

"Well?"

"Well, I probably ought to think you're crazy. But I don't. Maybe I'm crazy, too. Or maybe it's because I died once, myself. . . ."

"You started to tell me that, that first night—and then the car skidded. What happened?"

"When I was seven my appendix burst. I died on the operating table—and I went to a place like that meadow. I'll tell you the funny thing, though. I felt that rushing thing come at me, too—that huge thing you said came at you in the end. Only it actually reached me. And it wasn't dark or scary. It was white—beautiful light—and it had wonderful wings."

Gillian was staring. "Then what?"

"It sent me back. I didn't have any choice. It loved me, but I had to go back anyway. So—zoom—back down the tunnel, and pop, back into the body. I've never forgotten it. And, it's hard to explain, but I know it was *real*. I guess that's why I believe you."

"Then maybe you understand what I've got to do. I don't know what Angel really is. . . . I think he may be some kind of demon. But I've got to stop him. Exorcize him or whatever."

David took her by the arms. "You can't. You don't know how."

"But maybe Melusine does. It's either her or that guy Ash at the club. He seemed all right. The only down side is that I think he was a vampire."

David had stiffened. "I vote for the witch—"

"Me, too."

"—but I want you to wait for me. They'll let me out later this afternoon."

"I *can't*. David, it's for Tanya and Kim, too. Melusine might know how to cure them. Anyway, I'm certainly going to ask her. And I can't let any more time go by."

David pulled at his hair with the hand that wasn't hooked to the IV. "Okay. All right, give me five minutes, and we'll go together now."

"No."

He was looking at the IV as if figuring out how to undo it. "Yes. Just wait for me—"

Gillian blew him a kiss from the door and ran before he looked up.

He couldn't help her. You couldn't fight Angel in ordinary ways. All David would be was leverage in Angel's hands—a hostage—something to threaten to harm.

Gillian jogged out of the hospital and through the parking lot. She found the Geo.

Okay, now if Melusine would just be at the store. . . .

(You don't really want to do this, you know.)

Gillian slammed the car door closed. She sat up very straight, looking at nothing, as she fastened her seat belt and started the car.

(Listen, kid. You ain't never had a friend like me.)

Gillian pulled out of the parking lot.

(Come on, give me a break. We can at least talk about this, can't we? There are some things you don't understand.)

She couldn't listen to him. She didn't dare answer him. The last time, he'd hypnotized her somehow, made her relax and give up control to him. That couldn't happen again.

But she couldn't shut his voice out. She couldn't get away from it.

(And you can't love *him*. There are rules against it. I'm serious. You belong to the Night World now—you're not *allowed* to love a human. If they find out, they'll kill you both.)

(And what were you trying to do to us?) Damn, she'd answered him back. She wouldn't do that again.

(Not hurt you. It was only him I wanted. I could have slipped in as he slipped out. . . .)

Don't listen, Gillian told herself. There must be some way of blocking him, of keeping him out of her mind. . . .

She began to sing.

"DECK the halls with boughs of HOL-ly! Fa la la la la . . ."

He hadn't been able to hear her thoughts when she hummed before. It seemed to work, now, as long as she kept her mind on the lyrics. She sang Christmas carols. Loudly. The fast ones, like "God Rest Ye Merry, Gentlemen" and "Joy to the World," were best.

"The Twelve Days of Christmas" got her the last few miles to Woodbridge.

Please be there. . . .

"FIVE gold-en rings," she caroled, hurrying into the Woodbridge Five and Ten with the shoe box under her arm. She didn't care who thought she was crazy. *"FOUR calling birds, THREE French hens . . ."*

She was at the door to the back room.

"TWO turtle doves . . ."

A very startled Melusine looked up from behind the counter.

"And a . . . please, you've got to help me! I've got this Angel who's trying to kill people!" She broke off the song and rushed to Melusine.

"You've . . . what?"

"I've got this—angel thing. And I can't stop him from

talking to me. . . ." Gillian suddenly realized that Angel *had* stopped talking. "Maybe he got scared when I came in here. But I still need your help. Please." Suddenly her eyes were stinging with tears again.

Melusine leaned both elbows on the counter and rested her chin on her hands. She looked surprised, but willing. "Why don't you tell me about it?"

For the second time that day, Gillian told her story. All of it. She hoped that by telling everything, she could make Melusine understand her urgency. And her lack of experience.

"So I'm not even a real witch," she said at the end.

"Oh, you're a witch, all right," Melusine said. There was color in her cheeks and a look of fascination in her dark eyes. "He told you the truth about that. Everybody knows about the lost Harman babies. Little Elspeth—the records say that she died in England. But obviously she didn't. And you're her descendant."

"Which means it's okay for me to do spells?"

Melusine laughed. "It's okay for anyone to do spells who *can* do spells. In my opinion. Some people don't feel the same way—"

"But can you help me take the spells *off*?" Gillian opened the shoe box. She felt ashamed to show the dolls to Melusine—even though she'd bought them here. "I wouldn't have done it if I'd known," she murmured feebly, as Melusine looked at the dolls.

"I know." Melusine gestured at her to be quiet. Gillian watched tensely and waited for the verdict.

"Okay, it looks as if you've started the process already. But I think . . . maybe some healing salve . . . and blessed thistle . . ."

She bustled around, almost flying in her chair. She applied things to the dolls. She asked Gillian to concentrate with her, and she said words Gillian didn't recognize.

Finally, she wrapped the wax dolls in what looked like white silk, and put them back in the box.

"Is that all? It's done?"

"Well, I think it's a good idea to keep the dolls, just in case we need to do more healing. Then, after that, we can unname them and get rid of them."

"But now Tanya and Kim will be okay?" Gillian was anxious for reassurance, and she couldn't help the quick glance of doubt she cast—at Melusine's missing leg.

Melusine was direct. "If they've had anything amputated, it won't cure them. We can't grow new limbs." She touched her leg. "*This* happened in a boating accident. But otherwise, yes, they should get better."

Gillian let out a breath she seemed to have been holding for hours. She shut her eyes. "Thanks. Thank you, Melusine. You don't know how good it feels to *not* feel like you're maiming somebody."

Then she opened her eyes. "But the hard part's still to come."

"'Angel.'"

"Yes."

"Well, I think you're right about it being hard." She looked Gillian straight in the eye. "And dangerous."

"I know that already." Gillian turned and took a quick pace around the room. "He can get into my mind and make me do things—"

"Not just your mind. Anyone's."

"And I'm pretty sure he can move objects by himself. Make cars skid. And he sees *everything*." She came back to the counter. "Melusine—what *is* he? And why's he doing all this? And why to *me*?"

"Well, the last question's the easiest. Because you died." Melusine wheeled quickly to a bookshelf at the end of the counter. She pulled down a volume.

"He must have caught you in the between-place, the place between earth and the Other Side. The place where *he* was," she said, wheeling back. "He pretended to be the welcomer, the one who guides you to the Other Side. That thing rushing at you at the end—that was probably the *real* welcomer. But this 'Angel' got you out of the between-place before it could reach you."

Gillian spoke flatly. "He's not a real angel, is he?"

"No."

Gillian braced herself. "Is he a devil?"

"I don't think so." Melusine's voice was gentle. She opened

the book, flipping pages. "From the way you brought him back with you, I think he must be a spirit. There are two ways of getting spirits from the between-place: you can summon them or you can go fetch them yourself. You did it the hard way."

"Wait a minute. You're saying I *brought* him?"

"Well, not consciously. I'm sure you didn't mean to. It sounds like he just sort of grabbed on and whooshed down the tunnel—what we call the narrow path—right along with you. Spirits in the between-place can watch us, sometimes talk to us, but they can't really interact with us. When you brought him to earth, you set him free to interact."

"Oh, wonderful," Gillian whispered. "So on top of everything, it's my fault from the beginning." She looked around dazedly, then back at Melusine. "But what *is* a spirit, really? A dead person?"

"An unhappy dead person." Melusine turned pages. "'An earthbound spirit is a damaged soul. . . .'" She shut the book. "Look, it's actually simple. When a spirit is *really* unhappy—when they've done something awful, or they've died with unfinished business—then they don't go on to the Other Side. They get stuck in—well, the book calls it 'the astral planes near earth.' *We* call it the between-place."

"Stuck."

"They won't go on. They're too angry and hopeless to even want to be healed. And they can do awful things to living people if they get down here, just out of general miserableness."

"But how do you get *rid* of them?"

Melusine drew a breath. "Well, that's the hard part. You can send them back to the between-place—*if* you have some blood and hair from their physical body. And *if* you have all sorts of special ingredients, which I can't get. And *if* you have the right spell, which I don't know."

"I see."

"And in any case, that only traps him in the between-place again. It doesn't heal him. But, Gillian, there's something I've got to tell you." Melusine's face was very serious, and she spoke almost formally. "You may not need to rely on me."

"What do you mean?"

"Gillian . . . I don't think you really understand who you are. Did he—this spirit—explain to you just *how* important the Harmans are?"

"He said Elspeth's sister was some big witch leader."

"The biggest. She's *the* Crone, the leader of all the witches. And the Harmans are—well, they're sort of like the royal family to us."

Gillian smiled bleakly. "So I'm a witch princess?"

"You told me that Elspeth is your mother's mother's mother. You're descended entirely through the female line from her. But that's—extraordinary. There are almost no Harman girls left. There were only *two* in the world—and now there's you. Don't you see, if you let the Night World know about this, they'll flock to help you. *They'll* take care of Angel."

Gillian was unimpressed. "And how long will that take?"

"For them to gather and everything . . . check out your family, make all the preparations . . . I don't know. It could probably be done in a matter of weeks."

"Too long. *Way* too long. You don't know what Angel can do in a few weeks."

"Then you can try to do it yourself."

"But how?"

"Well, you'd have to find out who he was as a person and what business he left unfinished. Then you'd have to finish it. And finally, you'd have to convince him to go on. To be willing to leave the between-place for the Other Side." She glanced wryly at Gillian. "I told you it would be hard."

"And I don't think he'd be very cooperative. He wouldn't *like* it."

"No. He could hurt you, Gillian."

Gillian nodded. "It doesn't matter. It's what I've got to do."

CHAPTER 15

Melusine was watching her. "You're strong. I think you can do it, daughter of Hellewise."

"I'm not strong. I'm *scared*."

"I think it may be possible to be both," Melusine said wryly. "But, Gillian? If you do get through it, please come back. I want to talk to you about some things. About the Night World—and about something called Circle Daybreak."

The way she said it alarmed Gillian. "Is it important?"

"It could be very important to you, a witch with human ancestors and surrounded by humans."

"Okay. I'll come back—if." Gillian glanced once around the shop. Maybe there was some sort of talisman or something she should take. . . .

But she knew she was just stalling. If there were anything helpful, Melusine would have already given it to her.

There was nothing left to do now but *go*.

"Good luck," Melusine said, and Gillian marched to the door. Not that she had any particular idea where she was going.

She was almost at the creaky front door of the Five and Ten when she heard Melusine calling.

"I forgot to mention one thing. Whoever your 'Angel' was, he was probably from this general area. Earthbound spirits usually hang around the place they died. Although that's probably not much help."

Gillian stood still, blinking. "No . . . no, it *is* helpful. It's great. It's given me an idea."

She turned and went through the door without really seeing it, stepped out into the square without really hearing the piped-in Christmas music.

At least I've got a place to go now, she thought.

She drove south, back toward Somerset, then took a winding road eastward into the hills. As she rounded a gentle curve she saw the cemetery spread out beneath her.

It was a very old graveyard, but still popular. Steeped in tradition, but with plenty of room. Grandpa Trevor was buried in the newer section, but there were ancient tombstones on the wooded hill.

If she had a chance of finding Angel, it might be here.

The only way to the older section was up a wooden staircase held in place by railway ties. Gillian climbed it cautiously, holding the handrail. Then she stood at the top and looked around, trying not to shiver.

She was among tall sycamores and oaks, which seemed to stretch black bony fingers in every direction. The sun was falling lower in the sky and long shadows tinged with lavender were reaching out from the trees.

Gillian braced herself. And then, as loudly as she could, she yelled.

"Come on, you! You know what I want!"

Silence.

Gillian refused to feel foolish. Gloved hands tucked under her arms, she shouted into the stillness.

"I know you can hear me! I know you're out there! The question is, are you in here?" She kicked a foot toward a snow-covered sandstone marker.

Because of course there was nothing she could do here on her own. The only way to get the information she needed, about who Angel had been in his earthly life and what he'd done or left undone, was from Angel himself.

Nobody else could tell her.

"Is this you?" Gillian scraped snow from a granite gravestone and read the words. "'Thomas Ewing, 1775, Who bled and Dy'd for Liberty.' Were you Thomas Ewing?"

The ice-coated twigs of the tree above her clashed together in the rising wind. It made a sound like a crystal chandelier.

"No, he sounds too brave. And you're obviously just a coward." She scraped some other stones. "Hey, maybe you were William Case. 'Cut down in the flower of Youth by falling from the Stagecoach.' That sounds more like you. Were you William Case?"

(Are you all finished singing?)

Gillian froze.

(Because I've got one for you.) The voice in her head began to sing raucously. Eerily. *(The Pha-a-antom of the Opera is here, inside your mind. . . .)*

"Oh, come on, Angel. You can do better than that. And why aren't you letting me see you? Too scared to meet me face to face?"

A light shimmered over the snow—a beautiful pale golden light that rippled like silk. It grew, it took on a shape.

And then Angel was standing there. Not floating. His feet actually seemed to touch the snow.

He looked—terrific. Haunting and beautiful in the gathering twilight. But his beauty was only frightening now. Gillian knew what was underneath it.

"Hi there," she almost whispered. "I guess you know what I'm here to talk about."

"Don't know and don't care. Should you be out here alone, anyway? Does anybody know where you are?"

Gillian positioned herself in front of him. She looked directly into eyes that were as violet and darkly luminous as the sky.

"I know what you are," she said, holding those eyes, giving every word equal weight. "Not an angel. Not a devil. You're just a person. Just like me."

"Wrong."

"You've got the same feelings as any other person. And you *can't* be happy being where you are. Nobody could. You can't *want* to be stuck there. If I were dead, I'd *hate* it."

The last words came out with a force that surprised even Gillian. Angel looked away.

An advantage. Gillian leapt in. "Hate it," she repeated. "Just *hanging* around, getting stagnant, watching other people living their lives. Being *nothing,* doing *nothing*—unless it's to make a little trouble for people on earth. What kind of a life is tha—" She broke off, realizing her mistake.

He was grinning maliciously, recovering. "No life!"

"All right, what kind of existence, then," Gillian said coldly. "You know what I mean. It stinks, Angel. It's putrid. It's disgusting."

A spasm crossed Angel's face. He whirled away from her. And for the first time since Gillian had seen him, she *saw* agitation in him. He was actually pacing, moving like a caged animal. And his hair—it seemed to be ruffled by some unseen wind.

Gillian pressed her advantage. "It's about as good as being under *there.*" She kicked at the dead weeds over a grave.

He whirled back, and his eyes were unnaturally bright. "But I *am* under there, Gillian."

For a moment, her skin prickled so that she couldn't speak. She had to force herself to say steadily, "Under that one?"

"No. But I'll show you where. Would you like that?" He

made a grand gesture, inviting her down the stairs. Gillian hesitated, then went, knowing he was behind her.

Her heart was pumping wildly. This was almost like a physical contest between them—a contest to see who could upset the other more.

But she had to do it. She had to make a *connection* with him. To reach into his anger and frustration and despair and somehow drag answers out of it.

And it *was* a contest. A contest of wills. Who could shout louder, who could be more merciless. Who could hold on.

The prize was Angel's soul.

She nearly tripped at the bottom of the stairs. It was too dark to see her footing. She noticed, almost absently, that it was getting very cold.

Something like an icy wind went past her—and there was light in front of her. Angel was walking there, not leaving any footprints in the snow. Gillian staggered after him.

They were heading for the newer section of the cemetery. Past it. Into the *very* new section.

"Here." Angel said. He turned. His eyes were glittering. He was standing behind a gravestone and his own light illuminated it.

Chills washed over Gillian.

This was what she had asked for, it was exactly what she had asked for. But it still made the hair on her neck stand on end.

He was under here. Right here. Beneath the ground. The body of the person she'd loved and trusted . . . whose voice had been the last thing she'd heard at night and the first thing each morning.

He was under here in some kind of box, unless maybe that had rotted. And he wasn't smiling and golden-haired and handsome. And she was going to find out his name from a stone.

"I'm here, Gillian," Angel said ghoulishly, leaning over the granite marker, resting his elbows on it. "Come up and say hello." He was smiling, but his eyes looked as if he hated her. Wild and reckless and bitter. Capable of anything.

And somehow, the sick horror that had been sweeping through Gillian disappeared.

Her eyes were full, spilling over. The tears froze on her cheeks. She brushed at them absently and knelt beside the grave, not on it. She didn't look at Angel.

She put her hands together for just a moment and bent her head. It was a wordless prayer to whatever Power might be out there.

Then she took off her glove and gently scraped snow away from the marker with her bare hand.

It was a simple granite headstone with a scrolled top. It read "In loving memory. Our son. Gary Fargeon."

"Gary Fargeon," Gillian said softly. She looked up at the figure leaning over the stone. "Gary."

He gave a mocking laugh, but it sounded forced. "Nice to

meet you. I was from Sterback; we were practically neighbors."

Gillian looked back down. The date of birth was eighteen years ago. And the date of death was the previous year.

"You died last year. And you were only seventeen."

"I had a little car crash," he said. "I was extremely drunk." He laughed again, wildly.

Gillian sat back on her heels. "Oh, really. Well, that was brilliant," she whispered.

"What's life?" He bared his teeth. "'Out, out, brief candle'— or something like that."

Gillian refused to be distracted. "Is *that* what you did?" she asked quietly. "Got yourself killed? Is that unfinished business somehow?"

"Wouldn't you like to know?" he said.

Okay, retreat. He wasn't ready yet. Maybe try some feminine wiles. "I just thought you trusted me—Angel. I thought we were supposed to be soulmates . . ."

"But by now you know we aren't, don't you? Because you found your real love—that jerk." Gary turned up the brilliance of his smile. "But even if we're not soulmates, we *are* connected, you know. We're cousins. Distant, but the bond is there."

Gillian's hands fell to her sides. She stared up at him. Lights were going on in her brain, but she wasn't quite sure what they illuminated yet.

The strangest thing was that she wasn't entirely surprised.

"Didn't you ever wonder why we both have the same color

eyes?" He stared down at her. Although everything was dark around him, his eyes were like violet flame. "I mean, it isn't exactly common. Your great-grandmother Elspeth had these eyes. So did her twin brother, Emmeth."

Twins.

Of course. The lost Harman *babies*, Melusine had said. Elspeth and Emmeth. "And you're . . ."

He smirked. "I'm Emmeth's great-grandson."

Now Gillian could see what her mind was trying to illuminate. Her thoughts were racing. "You're a witch, too. That was why you knew how to do the spells and things. But how did you figure out what you were?"

"Some idiots from Circle Daybreak came," Gary said. "They were looking for lost witches. They'd managed to track Emmeth's descendants down. They told me enough that I understood what kind of powers I had. And then—I told them to get lost themselves."

"*Why?*"

"They were jerks. All they care about is getting humans and Night People together. But I knew the Night World was the place for me. Humans deserve what they get."

Gillian stood. Her fingers were getting red and swollen. She tried to pull her glove back on. "Gary, you *are* a human. At least part. Just like I am."

"No. We're superior to them. We're special—"

"We are *not* special. We're no better than anyone else!"

Gary was grinning unpleasantly, breathing quickly. "You're wrong there. The Night People are supposed to be *hunters*. There are even laws that say so."

A chill that had nothing to do with the wind went through Gillian. "Oh, really?" Then she had another thought. "Is *that* why you made me go to that club? So they could hunt *me*?"

"No, you idiot!" Gary's eyes flashed. "I told you—you're one of them. I just wanted you to *realize* that. You could have stayed, been part of them—"

"But *why*?"

"So you would be like *me*!" The wind was gusting wildly again. Frozen tree branches creaked like creatures in pain.

"But why?"

"So you could come be *with* me. So we could be together. Forever. If you joined them, you wouldn't have gone on to the Other Side—"

"When I died! You wanted me dead."

Gary looked confused. "That was just at first—"

Gillian was angry now. Yelling. "You planned the whole thing! You *lured* me. Didn't you? Didn't you? That crying I heard in the woods—that was you, wasn't it?"

"I—"

"Everything you did was designed to kill me! Just so you'd have company!"

"I was lonely!" The words seemed to hang and echo. Then Gary's eyes darkened and he turned away.

"I was so lonely," he said again, and there was something so hopeless in his voice that Gillian stepped toward him.

"Anyway, I didn't do it," he said over his shoulder. "I changed my mind. I thought I could come live with you here—"

"By killing David and taking his body. Yeah. Great plan."

He didn't move. Helplessly, Gillian reached out a hand. It passed right through his shoulder.

She looked at the hand, then said quietly, "Gary, tell me what you did. What the unfinished business is."

"So you can try to send me on."

"Yes."

"But what if I don't want to *go* on?"

"You have to!" Gillian clenched her teeth. "You don't *belong* here, Gary! This isn't your place anymore! And there's nothing you can do here, except . . . except *evil.*" She stopped, breathing hard.

He turned, and she saw the wild look again. "Maybe that's what I *like* to do."

"You don't understand. *I'm not going to let you.* I'm not going to stop or give up. I'll do whatever it takes to make you move on."

"But maybe you won't have the chance."

A blast of wind. And something else. Stinging granules that struck Gillian's face like tiny needles.

"What if there's a blizzard tonight?"

"Gary, stop it!" The gale buffeted her.

"A freak storm. Something nobody expected."

"Gary . . ." It was very dark—the moon and stars had been blotted out. But Gillian could see a driving, swirling whiteness. Her teeth were chattering and her face was numb.

"And what if Amy's car won't start? If something went wrong with the engine . . ."

"Don't do this! Gary!" She couldn't see him now. His light was gone, swallowed in the storm. Snow slashed her face.

"Nobody knows where you are, do they? That wasn't very smart, dragonfly. Maybe you need somebody to look after you, after all."

Gillian gasped, openmouthed, for breath. She tried to take a step and the wind thrust her against something hard. A tombstone.

This was what she'd been afraid of. That her angel would turn against her, try to destroy her. But now that it was happening, she found that she knew what to do.

Gary's voice came out of the gale. "What if I just go away and leave you for a little while?"

Gillian's eyes were watering, the tears freezing on her lashes. It was hard to get a breath. But she gathered herself, hanging on to the tombstone, and yelled.

"You won't! You *know* you won't—"

"How can I know?"

She answered with a question, shouting over the wind. "Why didn't you kill David?"

Her only answer was the howling gale.

Gillian's sight was dimming. The cold *hurt*. She tried to cling on to the tombstone, but her hands were numb. "You couldn't do it, Gary! You couldn't kill someone! When it came right down to it, you couldn't! And that's how I know."

She waited. At first she thought that she'd been wrong. That he'd left her alone in the storm.

Then she realized the wind was dying. The curtains of snow were thinning. Stopping. A light formed in the empty air.

Angel—no, Gary—was standing there. She could see him clearly. She could even see what was in his eyes.

Bitterness. Anger. But something like a plea, too.

"But I did, Gillian. That's exactly what I did. I killed someone."

Gillian took a breath that started out quick and ended long. Oh. Oh . . . that was bad.

But there might have been some justification. A fight. Self-defense.

She said quietly, "Who?"

"Can't you guess? Paula Belizer."

CHAPTER 16

Gillian stood as if her snow-powdered body had been turned to ice. Because it was the worst, the absolute worst that she could possibly have imagined.

He killed a kid.

"The little girl who disappeared a year ago," she whispered. "On Hillcrest Road." The one she'd thought of—completely irrationally—when she'd heard the crying.

"I was doing a spell," Gary said. "A strong one; I was a quick learner. It was a fire elemental spell—so I was out in the woods. In the snow, where nothing would burn. And then she showed up chasing her dog."

He was staring into the distance, his face dead white. Looking not haunting, but haunted. And Gillian knew he wasn't with her at that moment; he was far away, with Paula.

"They broke the circle. It all happened so fast. The fire was everywhere—just one white flash, like lightning. And then it was gone." He paused. "The dog got away. But not her."

Gillian shut her eyes, trying not to imagine it. "Oh, God." And then, as something twisted inside her, "Oh, Gary . . ."

"I put her body in my car. I was going to take her to the hospital. But she was *dead*. And I was—confused. So finally I stopped the car. And I buried her in the snow."

"Gary . . ."

"I went home. Then I went to a party. That was the kind of guy I was, you see. A partyin' guy. Everything was about good times and me, me, me. That was even what being a witch was about." For the first time there was emotion in his voice, and Gillian recognized it. Self-hatred.

"And at the party, I got really, really drunk."

Oh. Suddenly Gillian understood. "You never told anybody."

"On the way back home I wrapped my car around a tree. And that was it." He laughed, but it wasn't a laugh. "Suddenly I'm in Neverland. Can't talk to anybody, can't touch anybody, but sure can see *everything*. I watched the search for her, you know. They passed about a foot away from her body."

Gillian gulped and looked away. Something had twisted and broken inside her, some idea of justice that would never be put back together. But this was no time to think about that.

It hadn't really been his fault . . . but what did that matter? You played the hand you got dealt. And Gary had played his badly. He'd started out with everything—good looks, obvious brains, and witch power enough to choke a horse—and he'd blown it.

Didn't matter. They had to go on from here.

She looked up at him. "Gary, you have to tell me where she is."

Silence.

"Gary, don't you see? That's your unfinished business. Her family doesn't know . . ." Gillian stopped and swallowed. When she went on, her voice wobbled. "Whether she's alive or dead. Don't you think they ought to *know* that?"

A long pause. Then he said, like a stubborn child, "I don't want to go anywhere."

Like a frightened child, Gillian thought. But she didn't look away from him. "Gary, they deserve to know," she said softly. "Once they're at peace—"

He almost shouted, "What if there isn't any peace for *me*?"

Not frightened, terrified.

"What if there isn't anywhere for me to go? What if they won't *take* me?"

Gillian shook her head. Her tears overflowed again. And she didn't have any answers for him. "I don't know. But it doesn't change what we've got to do. I'll stay with you, though, if you want. I'm your cousin, Gary." Then, very quietly, she said, "Take me to her."

He stood for a long moment—the longest of Gillian's life.

He was looking at something in the night sky that she couldn't see, and his eyes were utterly bleak.

Then he looked at her and slowly nodded.

"Here?" David bent and touched the snow. He looked up at Gillian. His dark eyes were young—a little scared. But his jaw was set.

"Yes. Right there."

"It's a pretty strange place to do it."

"I know. But we don't have any choice."

David got to work with the shovel. Gillian pushed and mounded snow into walls. She tried to think only of how she'd done this in childhood, about how easy and interesting it had been then. She kept at it until David said, "I found her."

Gillian stepped back, brushing off her sleeves and mittens.

It was a clear day, and the afternoon sun was brilliant in a cold blue sky. The small clearing was peaceful, almost a haven. Untouched except for a welt in the snow where a ground mouse had tunneled.

Gillian took a couple of deep breaths, fists clenched, and then she turned to look.

David hadn't uncovered much. A scrap of charred red wool muffler. He was kneeling beside the shallow trench he'd made.

Gillian was crying again. She ignored it. She said, "It was the last day before Christmas vacation, so we took the day off from school. We were playing hooky in the woods. We decided to make a snow fort. . . ."

"And then we found the body." David got up and gently put a hand on her elbow. "It's a weird story, but it's better than the truth."

"And what can they suspect us of? We never even knew Paula Belizer. They'll know she was murdered because she was buried. But they won't know how she died. They'll think somebody tried to burn the body to get rid of it."

David put his arm around her waist, and she leaned into him. They stood that way for a few minutes, steadying each other.

It was strange how natural that was, now. David had agreed to help her with all this without a moment's hesitation . . . and Gillian hadn't been surprised. She'd expected it. He was her soulmate. They stood together.

At last, he said quietly, "Ready?"

"Yes."

As they left the clearing, David added even more quietly, "Is he here?"

"No. I haven't seen him since he showed me the place. He just—disappeared. He won't talk to me either."

David held her tighter.

Mr. Belizer came at dusk, after most of the police had left.

It was almost too dark to see. David had been urging Gillian away for an hour. So had Gillian's parents. They were there, both of them, huddling close and touching her whenever they could. David's father and stepmother were on the other side of David.

Yeah, Gillian thought. It's been a rough last few days on everybody.

But here they all were: David, pale but calm; Gillian, shaky but standing; the parents, bewildered but trying to cope. Not comprehending how their kids could have found so much trouble in such a short time.

At least nobody seemed to suspect them of having hurt Paula Belizer.

And now, here was Paula's dad. Alone. Come to look at the last resting place of his daughter—even though the coroner had already taken his daughter away.

The police let him go up to the clearing with a flashlight.

Gillian tugged at David's hand.

He resisted a second, then let her tow him. Gillian heard murmurs as they went. What are you doing, following that poor man. My God, that's—ghoulish. But none of the parents actually grabbed them to stop them.

They ended up a little distance behind Mr. Belizer. Gillian moved to see his face.

Now here was the thing. She didn't know about spirits. She wasn't sure *what* needed to be done to release Gary from the between-place. Did she need to talk to Paula's dad? Explain that she had the feeling whoever had done it was sorry, even if they could never tell him themselves?

It might get her locked up. Showing too much interest in a crime, too much knowledge. But, strangely, that didn't scare her as much as she'd have thought. She was Gary's cousin, and his debts were hers somehow. And things had to be put right.

As she stood hesitating, Mr. Belizer fell to his knees in the trampled snow.

Oh, God. That hurt. If strong arms hadn't been holding Gillian up, she might have fallen, too.

David held her and pressed his face into her hair. But Gillian kept looking at the kneeling man.

He was crying. She'd never seen a man his age cry, and it hurt in a way that was *scary*. But there was something else in his face. Something like relief . . . peace.

Kneeling there, with his overcoat spread around him, Mr. Belizer said, "I know my daughter is in a better place. Whoever did this, I forgive them."

A shock like cold lightning went through Gillian, and then a spreading warmth. She was crying suddenly. Hard. Tears falling straight down from her eyes. But she was filled with a hope that seemed to lift her whole body.

And then David drew in his breath sharply, and she realized he'd raised his head. He was staring at something above Mr. Belizer.

Gary Fargeon was hovering there. Like an Angel.

He was crying. And saying something over and over. Gillian caught "—sorry, I'm so sorry. . . ."

Forgiveness asked for and given. If not exactly in that order.

That's it, Gillian thought. Her knees began to tremble.

David whispered huskily, "Can you see that, too?"

"Yes. Can you?"

Nobody else seemed to see it. Mr. Belizer was getting up now. He was walking past them, away.

David was still staring. "So that's what he looks like. No wonder you thought—"

He didn't finish, but Gillian knew. Thought he was an angel.

But . . . why was Gary still here? Wasn't the forgiveness enough to release him? Or was there something else that needed to be done?

Gary turned his head and looked at her. His cheeks were wet. "Come in a little farther," he said. "I have to say something."

Gillian untangled from David, and then pulled at him. He came, jaw still sagging. They followed Gary past a thicket and into another clearing. As the trees and the darkness closed around them, they seemed suddenly far away from the police noise and bustle.

Gillian guessed even as Gary sank down to face them. But she let him say it.

"You have to forgive me, too."

"I forgive you," Gillian said.

"You have to be sure. I did some terrible things to you. I tried to warp you, damage your soul."

"I know," Gillian said steadily. "But you did some good things, too. You helped me—grow up."

He'd helped her conquer her fears. Gain self-confidence. Discover her heritage. And find her soulmate.

And he'd been close to her in a way that she would probably never be with anyone else ever again.

"You know what?" Gillian was on the verge of tears again. "I'm going to miss you."

He stood facing her. He was shining just dimly. His eyes were dark and bruised-looking, but his lips were smiling. And he was more beautiful than she had ever seen him.

"Things are going to work out, you know," he said softly. "For you. Your mom's going to get better."

Gillian nodded. "I think so, too."

"And I checked on Tanya and Kim. They're going to be all right. Tanya's still got all her fingers."

"I know."

"You should go see Melusine. You could help them a lot with Circle Daybreak. And they can help you deal with the Night World."

"Yes. All right."

"And you might want to talk to Daryl at school. She's got a secret that Kim was spreading rumors about last year. It's that—"

"Ang—Gary!" Gillian held up her hand. "I don't want to know. Someday, if Daryl wants to tell me her secret, she can do it herself. But if not—okay. I have to deal on my own, now."

She'd already thought about school, all last night while she'd been lying alone in her room. Things were going to change, obviously. It was surprisingly easy to sort out which friends mattered.

Amanda the Cheerleader and Steffi the Singer and J. Z. the Model were all right. No better and no worse than any of the less popular girls. She wouldn't mind if they still liked her.

Daryl—who was not Daryl the Rich Girl anymore, but just Daryl—was better than all right. The sort that might turn out to be a real friend. And of course there was Amy. She owed Amy a lot.

As for the others—Tanya and Kim and Cory and Bruce and Macon—Gillian didn't really *want* to know them. If she never went to another Popular Party, that was fine.

"And I don't want to know if J. Z. really tried to kill herself, either," she said now.

Gary shut his mouth. Then his eyes actually seemed to twinkle. "You're going to do all right." And then, for the first time, he looked at David.

They stared at each other for a moment. Not hostile. Just looking.

When Gary turned back to Gillian he said very quietly, "One last thing. I didn't change my mind about killing him because I couldn't go through with it. I did it because I didn't want you to hate me forever."

Oh.

Gillian put out her hand. So did he. Their fingers were close together, blurring into each other . . . but they couldn't touch. They never would.

And then suddenly, Gary looked startled. He turned to look up and behind him.

At the dark, starlit sky.

Gillian couldn't see anything. But she could *feel* something. A sort of rushing. Something was coming.

And Gary was lifted toward it like a leaf on the wind.

His hand was still stretched toward her, but he was in the air. Weightless. Bobbing. And as Gillian watched, his startled expression melted into something like awe.

And then joy. Joy and . . . recognition.

"I've got to go," he said wonderingly.

Gillian was staring at the sky. She still couldn't see anything. Not the tunnel, not the meadow. Did he mean he had to go to the between-place?

And then she saw the light.

It was the color of sunlight on snow. That brilliant, but not painful to look at. It seemed to shimmer with every color in the universe, but all together the colors made white.

"Gary—"

But something was happening. He was moving without

moving. Rushing away in some direction she couldn't point to. Getting smaller. Fading. She was losing him.

"Goodbye, Gary," she whispered.

And the light was going, too. But just before it went, it seemed to take on a shape. It looked something like huge white wings enfolding him.

For the briefest instant, Gillian felt enfolded, too. By power and peace . . . and love.

And then the light was gone. Gary was gone. And everything was still.

"Did you see that?" Gillian whispered through the ache in her throat.

"I think so." David was staring, his eyes big with awe and wonder.

"Maybe . . . some angels are real."

He was still staring upward. Then he drew in his breath. "Look! The stars—"

But it wasn't stars, although it looked like stardust. Crystalline points of light, frozen beauty sifting down. The air was full of it.

"But there aren't any clouds. . . ."

"There are now," David said. Even as he said it, the stars were covered. Gillian felt a cool touch on her cheek.

Like a kiss.

And it was ordinary snow, just an ordinary miracle. She and David stood hand in hand, watching it fall like a blessing in the night.

The Night World
lives on in *The Chosen*,
by L. J. Smith.

I t happened at Rashel's birthday party, the day she turned five years old.

"Can we go in the tubes?" She was having her birthday at a carnival and it had the biggest climbing structure of tubes and slides she had ever seen.

Her mother smiled. "Okay, kitten, but take care of Timmy. He's not as fast as you are."

They were the last words her mother ever said to her.

Rashel didn't have to be told, though. She always took care of Timmy: he was a whole month younger than she was, and he wasn't even going to kindergarten next year. He had silky black hair, blue eyes, and a very sweet smile. Rashel had dark hair, too, but her eyes were green—green as emeralds, Mommy always said. Green as a cat's.

As they climbed through the tubes she kept glancing back at him, and when they got to a long row of vinyl-padded stairs—slippery and easy to slide off of—she held out a hand to help him up.

Timmy beamed at her, his tilted blue eyes shining with adoration. When they had both crawled to the top of the stairs, Rashel let go of his hand.

She was heading toward the spiderweb, a big room made entirely of rope and net. Every so often she glanced through a fish-bowl window in one of the tubes and saw her mother waving at her from below. But then another mother came to talk to hers and Rashel stopped looking out. Parents never seemed to be able to talk and wave at the same time.

She concentrated on getting through the tubes, which smelled like plastic with a hint of old socks. She pretended she was a rabbit in a tunnel. And she kept an eye on Timmy—until they got to the base of the spiderweb.

It was far in the back of the climbing structure. There were no other kids around, big or little, and almost no noise. A white rope with knots at regular intervals stretched above Rashel, higher and higher, leading to the web itself.

"Okay, you stay here, and I'll go up and see how you do it," she said to Timmy. This was a sort of fib. The truth was that she didn't think Timmy could make it, and if she waited for him, neither of them would get up.

"No, I don't want you to go without me," Timmy said. There was a touch of anxiety in his voice.

"It's only going to take a second," Rashel said. She knew

what he was afraid of, and she added, "No big kids are going to come and push you."

Timmy still looked doubtful. Rashel said thoughtfully, "Don't you want ice cream cake when we get back to my house?"

It wasn't even a veiled threat. Timmy looked confused, then sighed heavily and nodded. "Okay. I'll wait."

And those were the last words Rashel heard *him* say.

She climbed the rope. It was even harder than she'd thought it would be, but when she got to the top it was wonderful. The whole world was a squiggly moving mass of netting. She had to hang on with both hands to keep her balance and try to curl her feet around the rough quivering lengths of cable. She could feel the air and sunlight. She laughed with exhilaration and bounced, looking at the colored plastic tubes all around her.

When she looked back down for Timmy, he was gone.

Rashel's stomach tensed. He *had* to be there. He'd promised to wait.

But he wasn't. She could see the entire padded room below the spiderweb from here, and it was empty.

Okay, he must have gone back through the tubes. Rashel made her way, staggering and swaying, from one handhold to another until she got to the rope. Then she climbed down quickly and stuck her head in a tube, blinking in the dimness.

"Timmy?" Her voice was a muffled echo. There was no

answer and what she could see of the tube was empty. "Timmy!"

Rashel was getting a very bad feeling in her stomach. In her head, she kept hearing her mother say, *Take care of Timmy.* But she hadn't taken care of him. And he could be anywhere by now, lost in the giant structure, maybe crying, maybe getting shoved around by big kids. Maybe even going to tell her mother.

That was when she saw the gap in the padded room.

It was just big enough for a four-year-old or a very slim five-year-old to get through. A space between two cushiony walls that led to the outside. And Rashel knew immediately that it was where Timmy had gone. It was like him to take the quickest way out. He was probably on his way to her mother right now.

Rashel was a very slim five-year-old. She wiggled through the gap, only sticking once. Then she was outside, breathless in the dusty shade.

She was about to head toward the front of the climbing structure when she noticed the tent flap fluttering.

The tent was made of shiny vinyl and its red and yellow stripes were much brighter than the plastic tubes. The loose flap moved in the breeze and Rashel saw that anyone could just lift it and walk inside.

Timmy wouldn't have gone in *there*, she thought. It wouldn't be like him at all. But somehow Rashel had an odd feeling.

She stared at the flap, hesitating, smelling dust and popcorn in the air. I'm brave, she told herself, and sidled forward. She pushed on the tent beside the flap to widen the gap, and she stretched her neck and peered inside.

It was too dark to see anything, but the smell of popcorn was stronger. Rashel moved farther and farther until she was actually in the tent. And then her eyes adjusted and she realized that she wasn't alone.

There was a tall man in the tent. He was wearing a long light-colored trench coat, even though it was warm outside. He didn't seem to notice Rashel because he had something in his arms, and his head was bent down to it, and he was doing something to it.

And then Rashel saw what he was doing and she knew that the grown-ups had lied when they said ogres and monsters and the things in fairy-tale books weren't real.

Because the tall man had Timmy, and he was *eating* him.

Eating him or doing something with his teeth. Tearing and sucking. Making noises like Pal did when he ate his dog food.

For a moment Rashel was frozen. The whole world had changed and everything seemed like a dream. Then she heard somebody screaming and her throat hurt and she knew it was her.

And then the tall man *looked* at her.

He lifted his head and looked. And she knew that his face alone was going to give her nightmares forever.

Not that he was ugly. But he had hair as red as blood and eyes that shone gold, like an animal's. There was a light in them that was like nothing she had ever seen.

She ran then. It was wrong to leave Timmy, but she was too scared to stay. She wasn't brave; she was a baby, but she couldn't help it. She was still screaming as she turned around and darted through the flap in the tent.

Almost darted through. Her head and shoulders got outside and she saw the red plastic tubes rising above her—and then a hand clamped on the back of her Gymboree shirt. A big strong hand that stopped her in midflight. Rashel was as helpless as a baby kitten against it.

But just as she was dragged back into the tent she saw something. *Her mother.* Her mother was coming around the corner of the climbing structure. She'd heard Rashel screaming.

Her mother's eyes were big and her mouth was open, and she was moving fast. She was coming to save Rashel.

"Mommeeeeeeeeee!" Rashel screamed, and then she was back inside the tent. The man threw her to one side the way a kid at preschool would throw a piece of crumpled paper. Rashel landed hard and felt a pain in her leg that normally would have made her cry. Now she hardly noticed it. She was staring at Timmy, who was lying on the ground near her.

Timmy looked strange. His body was like a rag doll's—arms and legs flopped out. His skin was white. His eyes were staring straight up at the top of the tent.

There were two big holes in his throat, with blood all around them.

Rashel whimpered. She was too frightened to scream anymore. But just then she saw white daylight, and a figure in front of it. Mommy. Mommy was pulling the tent flap open. Mommy was inside, looking around for Rashel.

That was when the worst thing happened. The worst and the strangest, the thing the police never believed when Rashel told them later.

Rashel saw her mother's mouth open, saw her mother looking at her, about to say something. And then she heard a voice—but it wasn't Mommy's voice.

And it wasn't an out-loud voice. It was inside her head.

Wait! There's nothing wrong here. But you need to stand very, very still.

Rashel looked at the tall man. His mouth wasn't moving, but the voice was his. Her mother was looking at him, too, and her expression was changing, becoming relaxed and . . . stupid. Mommy was standing very, very still.

Then the tall man hit Mommy once on the side of the neck and she fell over and her head flopped the wrong way like a broken doll. Her dark hair was lying in the dirt.

Rashel saw that and then everything was even more like a dream. Her mother was dead. Timmy was dead. And the man was looking at her.

You're not upset, came the voice in her head. *You're not frightened. You want to come right here.*

Rashel could feel the pull of the voice. It was drawing her closer and closer. It was making her still and not afraid, making her forget her mother. But then she saw the tall man's golden eyes and they were *hungry.* And all of a sudden she remembered what he wanted to do to her.

Not me!

She jerked away from the voice and dove for the tent flap again.

This time she got all the way outside. And she threw herself straight at the gap in the climbing structure.

She was thinking in a different way than she had ever thought before. The Rashel that had watched Mommy fall was locked away in a little room inside her, crying. It was a new Rashel who wiggled desperately through the gap in the padded room, a smart Rashel who knew that there was no point in crying because there was nobody who cared anymore. Mommy couldn't save her, so she had to save herself.

She felt a hand grab her ankle, hard enough almost to crush her bones. It yanked, trying to drag her back through the gap. Rashel kicked backward with all her strength and then twisted, and her sock came off and she pulled her leg into the padded room.

Come back! You need to come back right now!

The voice was like a teacher's voice. It was hard not to listen. But Rashel was already scrambling into the plastic tube in front of her. She went faster than she ever had before, hurting her knees, propelling herself with her bare foot.

When she got to the first fish-bowl window, though, she saw a face looking in at her.

It was the tall man. He was staring at her. He banged on the plastic as she went by.

Fear cracked in Rashel like a belt. She scrambled faster, and the knocks on the tube followed her.

He was underneath her now. Keeping up with her. Rashel passed another window and looked down. She could see his hair shining in the sunlight. She could see his pale face looking up at her.

And his eyes.

Come down, came the voice and it wasn't stern anymore. It was sweet. *Come down and we'll go get some ice cream. What kind of ice cream do you like best?*

Rashel knew then that this was how he'd gotten Timmy into the tent. She didn't even pause in her scrambling.

But she couldn't get away from him. He was traveling with her, just under her, waiting for her to come out or get to a place where he could reach in and grab her.

Higher. I need to get higher, she thought.

She moved instinctively, as if some sixth sense was telling her which way to turn each time she had a choice. She went through angled tubes, straight tubes, tubes that weren't solid at all, but made of woven canvas strips. And finally she got to a place where she couldn't go any higher.

It was a square room with a padded floor and netting sides. She was at the front of the climbing structure; she could see mothers and fathers standing and sitting in little groups. She could feel the wind.

Below her, looking up, was the tall man.

Chocolate brownie? Mint chip? Bubble gum?

The voice was putting pictures in her mind. Tastes. Rashel looked around frantically.

There was so much noise—every kid in the climbing structure was yelling. Who would even notice her if she shouted? They'd think she was joking around.

All you have to do is come down. You know you have to come down sometime.

Rashel looked into the pale face turned up to her. The eyes were like dark holes. Hungry. Patient. Certain.

He knew he was going to get her.